A LIFE
UNOPENED

KIM WILLIAMS

Memories of Shirley Kaye lie nestled in these lines.

A LIFE UNOPENED

Everyone should be missed by someone.

PROLOGUE

September 1944
Hazel, Texas

She closed the cover of the telephone phone book and wiped a tear. At the foot of the bed, her daughter slept, innocent of the horrendous fate awaiting her.

"Carol Ruth Mullins." She spoke her own name aloud, realizing it could fade into the vast unknown, never to be spoken again. Without loved ones to carry on the memories, a person's name dies with their body. Oh, perhaps passers-by in a graveyard would read the name on her tombstone with little interest as they walked to the resting place of a family member, but the name wouldn't linger in anyone's heart.

She glanced at her sweet girl—her loved one. Would this child forgive her one day? If so, would her name grace those rosy lips, now slightly parted in sleep's bliss? Would her child ever utter "Momma" without a tinge of pain in her heart?

It was not Carol's fate to know these things.

She slid the phone book into the drawer of the bedside table. Warped, the drawer squeaked as she pushed it closed. Having called every household with his last name listed in the directory, she felt defeated. None claimed him as kin. Some suggested names who may be related, but those names weren't listed in the directory. Her searching was done. She would do the inevitable.

Perhaps she'd been a fool not to go into an unwed mother's home. Her child may have been adopted and cared for by now. She'd been selfish, she supposed, bearing the shame of being unwed, giving birth by a midwife she paid with cash she'd saved, bringing up her child in the room she rented above the goods store where she worked. Hoping he would re-enter their lives.

Depleted by the travel to this town and by emotion, weariness enveloped her sick body. She ran her finger through dust on the table top. The motor lodge on the edge of Hazel, Texas, offered shelter with a hint of cleanliness.

Dust. Her soul would live on, but her body, racked with disease, would become dust. She blew the particles off her finger.

The child stirred beside her, and she bent to kiss the sweet cheeks, drinking in the tiny features and inhaling her scent. Once the toddler settled again, Carol pulled a paper tablet from her suitcase, and positioning herself against a headboard, began writing her daughter a letter.

Two hours later, she rose from her seat on the city bus, adjusting the child in her arms. As they moved down the aisle, the small girl smiled and waved "bye-bye" to those still seated. The lighthearted chuckles and returned waves mocked the truth of the impending goodbye. Carol sniffled and tried to keep her lip from quivering. Her sick body ached from the weight of the child, and her heart broke from the weight of the coming loss.

Ahead, to the right, the orphanage stood as the lone fixture against the nothingness of the black, flat Texas earth, as though it, too were outcast from society. The bus stop was situated between the border of grace and disgrace.

She crossed the road and trudged her way down the gravel sidewalk, heat beating on her neck and her feet unsteady in the pebbles. She hadn't the energy to sing, so she hummed her child's favorite lullaby. The girl touched her face, then rested her head against her shoulder, raising it when they entered the cold building. If Desperation had a home, this place was it.

A tall, young woman, stiff in posture but with gentle eyes, met her in the tiny waiting area.

"I'm Miss Bords, the assistant superintendent. I understand you have a child for us." The woman's gaze rested on her daughter.

"I do." Sobs wracked Carol's body. The room seemed to darken, and she felt suffocated.

The stiff woman relaxed her posture and leaned toward Carol. "Sit in this chair."

Carol sat and played with her daughter's hair until she could speak.

"I'm dying."

Miss Bords, sitting inches away, patted Carol's shoulder, who then spilled her story.

At last, Carol, emptied of words, handed the woman a large manila envelope.

"This is our story, when she is old enough to understand and desires to know. Please ask the adopting parents to honor my request."

"Of course."

Time can be gracious when it so chooses, for the moments blurred as she rendered her daughter.

Then Carol opened the front door to exit and heard her child's "bye-bye" explode into a wail.

As long as she lived, that moment would suffocate her.

Carol wept.

Truthfully, she was already dead. Her body just hadn't caught up.

1

Weddings and funerals intrigued her. People gathered in the name of love. Families celebrating or mourning one of their own. She was unpracticed in both ceremonies. Indeed, she lacked experience with any familial ritual or ruckus.

Marjorie wiped sweat from her brow, then shielded her eyes against the sun. Of course, the day her town set aside for the local soldier's memorial parade was the hottest September day on record. And, of course, she had forgotten to grab her sunglasses from her bunk.

A sparse gathering lined the street. The same street that housed the only home she'd ever known, Anderson Orphanage.

The same street that housed the local junior high.

She rolled her eyes. Whoever decided ten years ago to build the school across from the orphanage had been clueless to the horrors of junior high culture. Otherwise, they wouldn't have forced orphaned teens to make the brief, yet long, "walk of shame" between the locations. Elementary school hadn't offered mockery for the social status she and the other orphans received when they got into junior high. Her memories of the place across the street held little fondness.

At nineteen she would be leaving the orphanage where she'd grown up then worked as a clerk to the superintendent. Culture was changing how it handled its orphaned children, with the rise of them entering temporary private homes until they were adopted or aged out. Formerly funded by the Baptist Association, Anderson had been bought by a private organization and would become a group home for orphaned children who failed in numerous home placements.

Marjorie now had to find a place to live and start life on her own. How fortunate she was to be the recipient of the local beauty college's annual scholarship for 1960. She'd applied and pled a good case for why she needed the financial assistance. Her goal was to run her own shop.

Marjorie bounced on her heels. No need to replay the embarrassments of junior high. Teenage humiliation knelt to adult anticipation.

Beads of moisture escaped her ebony bob and rolled down her back. A breeze hurried through and swung hair onto her cheek. With one motion she swiped the strands and tucked them behind her ear. Heat made the small purse on her arm feel heavy. The orphanage superintendent and other staff stood near her, each ready to pay their respects when the military procession passed by.

Though comprised of 38 square miles, Hazel's population of 18,000 was spread over a rural area. Three elementary schools, a junior high, and a senior high housed its students. A small business district had grown to the west of downtown, and much to Marjorie's pleasure, Hazel housed a local beauty college.

She stood on the outskirts of the route that would proceed downtown toward the local cemetery. Though the crowd was sparse here, local news and radio suspected a large gathering in the heart of Hazel's downtown to pay their respects to the local WW2 soldier being laid to rest. According to the newspaper, the twenty-four-year old's remains had recently been found in Belgium and identified as local citizen Troy Darden.

Truth was, the Darden story stirred her. He had evolved from MIA to hero. How deeply had his family grieved all these years not knowing his fate? How must he have felt going off to war loved by others? She'd never felt the love of family. She supposed, too, that she'd never been missed.

Everyone should be missed by someone.

She looked across the street at the school yard. Teachers directed students as they formed groups strolling alongside each other on the sidewalk and settling into place class by class. Perhaps they had been instructed in proper etiquette for a funeral procession since most stood at attention with serious faces. They could be packaged dolls stuffed onto a shelf in the department store.

It was all Marjorie could do not to chuckle as she surveyed the class standing directly across the street from her. Oh, the unfairness of junior high development with its variety of shapes and heights. Most of the girls towered over the boys. The tallest of the boys moved from the back of the group to stand beside the front row. Marjorie's chuckle escaped. That figure was no student. The navy sport coat, gold tie, and clip board attested to his being a teacher. His face looked young, not much older than her own. A warmth moved inside her, and it had nothing to do with the heat. A man devoted to molding lives appealed to her. She'd never realized that fact.

"Stop staring." Though the voice was her own, Marjorie jumped at its sound. She pushed herself back into the seriousness of the occasion.

The sound of bagpipes captured her attention. The parade approached.

Six police officers on motorcycles led the procession, followed by a lone bagpipe player who filled the silence with *Amazing Grace*. The hearse came into view, displaying a casket draped with the American flag. A gentle motion flowed through the thin crowd as members of the armed forces raised their hand in salute while other male by-standers placed their hats over their hearts. Others watching, like herself, displayed handheld flags.

A black Cadillac followed the hearse. Only one car rode in the procession. A small family? Miniature flags attached to the vehicle waved in the breeze. The color guard came next, followed by junior and senior high school ROTC members. They marched behind the color guard in perfect precision. Two more motorcycle policemen marked the end of the procession.

Observers began to disperse while reverence kept the atmosphere quiet. Marjorie stepped off the sidewalk and crossed the street toward the city bus stop on the same side of the street as the school. She glanced at the watch she'd chosen for today, the silver one with a pale blue face. The piece was not expensive; none of her watches were. They were Christmas gifts from gracious donors who afforded Anderson orphans one wish at Christmas besides underclothing and socks.

She was pushing it to make her appointment with both the owner of Hillhurst Nursing Home and the owner of the beauty shop housed inside it. Surely, they would understand the slight delay caused by paying her last respects.

Within the hour, she could be employed as the assistant at the home's salon. She grinned. Such a nice title for someone who swept up hair, disinfected combs and brushes, and laundered towels. But she couldn't imagine a better job while she attended cosmetology school.

Ouch! Someone stepped on her foot. She looked up from checking the time to see the back of a young male. She braced a palm against him to steady herself. Perspiration saturated his light blue shirt. And no question the boy had not been introduced to deodorant. She held her breath.

The young teen turned to face her. Poor thing. His hormones created an unappealing bumpy display on his face. His voice squeaked out regret while his acne blended with the flush on his cheeks.

"Ma'am. I'm sorry."

"No worries."

Tell that to her aching toes on her size nine foot. Her right one had taken the force of his weight. The young man obviously hadn't outgrown his baby fat.

He turned and lugged himself to the back of a line of students. She hastened forward, but paused when she heard a controlled voice from behind.

The tone appealed to her. This was no teenager speaking.

"Rusty, what were you doing in the street? I told our class to stay on the sidewalk as we went back into the school."

She glanced over her shoulder. Mr. Good-Looking teacher stood facing the rotund teen she'd encountered.

"Yes sir, but Curtis bumped into me. I lost my balance and fell backward off the curb."

"Did you apologize to the lady?"

Perhaps you should chase me down to make sure he did.

"Yes, Mr. Buckler."

She rolled the name over her tongue. "Mr. Buckler." Nice.

Are you single?

Marjorie grinned then picked up her pace.

The handsome instructor no doubt had his hands full with junior high students.

And, not once in her lackluster junior high career had any teacher resembling Mr. Buckler ever written an assignment on the blackboard or chided a student for stepping out of line. If a teacher that handsome had passed her in the hall, Marjorie's awkward junior high self would have noticed.

• • •

Daniel tossed his chewed pencil into the trashcan. He really should break the nasty habit. The most recent number-two had outlasted its predecessor by a week before he decided it had too many teeth marks for his liking. Why did holding a pencil between his teeth help him think?

He fidgeted with the small flag on the corner of his desk. Every student and teacher had been offered one for the procession. He grinned. He'd suggested that to the principal at a teacher's meeting, then was assigned the task of getting them.

It hadn't been easy watching the limousine roll by at the procession. He couldn't serve his country as a soldier. His weak heart disqualified him from the military. His broken heart might have enjoyed the escape.

Most students seemed moved by the procession. He eyed the empty classroom and smiled. He loved it when history came alive for them.

Daniel sucked in a breath, realizing the irony of his thought. He'd meant no disrespect.

He closed his desk drawer and stared. A textbook lay on the first desk in the first row. What excuse would Curtis offer tomorrow for not completing the reading assignment?

Today he felt weary of Curtis. On the surface, the young man's life seemed near perfect for his age. Wealthy family. Good looks. Athletic.

Yet, Daniel reckoned he felt no true value, otherwise he wouldn't seek approval by shaming kids like Rusty who struggled socially. If Curtis and other students would take time to observe Rusty's character instead of his looks and odor, Daniel suspected they'd like him. Perhaps that was too much to expect at this age of maturity, or lack thereof.

He should talk to Rusty about his odor.

Rusty's family lived four houses down from his own childhood home here in Hazel. The boy's talents weren't of the athletic type. Nor did he possess an engaging personality. But for as long as Daniel had known Rusty, he'd been impressed with his depth of integrity and his good heart.

He hated to see junior high form that goodness into anger and sadness.

Daniel snapped his fingers as Purpose tapped him on the shoulder. That's why he taught junior high, to help kids like Rusty (and, yes, like Curtis) know they had value and purpose. The fact that Daniel loved teaching history was a bonus.

He whistled and pushed his wooden desk chair back. He should oil those squeaky wheels. Time to head home and spend the evening with his red pen and a TV dinner. Albeit, he wondered what a quiet evening in a fine restaurant with the funeral lady would be like. Funeral lady? Was that the best descriptor his mind could conjure up of the dark-haired woman Rusty had tripped onto?

He'd noticed her long before Rusty bumped in to her. He'd noted the emotional juxtaposition of focusing on the fallen while noticing the living. She'd stood there, shielding her eyes from the sun. He'd been struck by her appearance. The flipped ends of her black hair that had blown in the breeze were natural and attractive, unlike the teased hair most women preferred. He supposed she had no idea how stunning she looked in that pale blue dress.

Truth was, he'd wanted to thank Rusty and Curtis for the incident that allowed him a few more glances at her. But he'd managed to remain professional. So professional, that he hadn't taken time to introduce himself, which went against his instincts.

He had, however, in that brief moment, made a point to direct his eyes to her left hand and saw no ring there. Of course, that knowledge would do him little good if he never saw her again. Daniel wondered where she was off to when the procession ended. Perhaps she worked as a secretary in some nearby office or lived close by. Why else would she be in that particular spot on the procession route?

It would be nice to put his failed relationship behind him, meet someone, and marry. Red pen and papers could leave a man occupied, but lonely. The fact that he'd noticed another woman made him wonder if was ready to move on.

Funeral lady, is anyone waiting for you at home?

Daniel grabbed his leather briefcase and headed to the classroom door. He stopped and skimmed the room to see if he had forgotten anything. His framed landscape paintings that hung between maps, posters, and bookshelves might appear out of place in a history class, but they belonged in Room 264, making the place uniquely his.

He loosened his tie, flipped the light switch, and stepped into the hall. The door clicked behind him. He'd taken one step forward when his name filled the quiet after-school atmosphere.

"Mr. Buckler."

Daniel knew the voice before he spotted its owner, the assistant principal. *This can't be good.* Memories of the last few days scurried across his tired mind. No incidents came forward—unless today's mishap between Curtis and Rusty had made its way to the office.

Daniel turned and walked toward the toothpick figure with graying temples. "Afternoon, Mr. Crawley."

"Afternoon." The man cleared his throat.

"What can I do for you?" Daniel sucked in a long breath. The diesel scent of bus duty emanated from his captor.

"The eighth-grade holiday dance is in two months. There's a need for another teacher on the committee. Administration has selected you."

Daniel interpreted the meaning.

To be the gopher. The one to do the grunt work.

He pushed down a groan. Dadgum. That was the last thing he wanted to do. He calculated the date. *Ugh.* And, he had planned to display his art at a show in Austin the weekend of the dance.

Candace came to mind. She would have enjoyed being on the planning committee. The same way she had enjoyed planning their wedding. The same wedding she'd canceled.

And in the end, it was the wedding and best man she'd been in love with, not the groom.

2

"Congratulations, Miss Mullins. I look forward to having you in our shop." The owner of The Wright Do, Valene Wright, extended her hand to Marjorie. Her manicure was enviable. Mr. Hurst, the nursing home owner, stood alongside his desk. The three of them occupied most of the space in his boxy office.

Marjorie opened her mouth to reply, but Mr. Hurst's voice prevented it.

"Our residents consider a visit to The Wright Do one of their weekly highlights. I run this place to feel like family. I think you'll fit right in."

"Thank you, Mr. Hurst and Mrs…"

"Miss." The correction sounded flat and lifeless, as though the owner were bored with repeating it.

"Miss Wright." Marjorie felt her cheeks heat. "I cannot wait to start my job. I'm grateful you selected me."

"Your passion for this work seems obvious by what I've gathered in our interview." Miss Wright picked up a file on the desk and slid Marjorie's application into it. "I will see you in a couple of days." Marjorie grinned, feeling like a four-year-old with an ice cream cone.

"And I apologize that you had to wait on us to start the interview. I called the orphanage and left a message for you with the time change once we knew when the procession was scheduled."

"Oh, I didn't get it. That's okay. I was at the procession too. Sitting here settled my nerves."

"I'll have your white smock ready. Be sure to wear a black skirt. Your top needs to be comfortable, but it won't show. The shop opens at 8:00 A.M. on Saturday. You need to arrive an hour beforehand. I offer coffee and donuts to our clientele and staff on Saturdays." Miss Wright moved toward the door and Marjorie followed. Mr. Hurst skirted around them and held the door open.

"Oh, and Marjorie, invest in a pair of black or white nursing shoes if you can. You'll be glad you did at the end of your shifts."

"Yes Ma'am." *After my first paycheck.*

"I think you'll feel quite at home at The Wright Do. And please, call me Valene."

Marjorie's eyes moistened. The waterworks came from joy. Both the scholarship and a job filled her. Had she been deflated her entire life and not known it? She blinked to keep the fledgling tears intact.

Mr. Hurst returned to his desk. Marjorie watched as Miss Wright headed in the direction she'd indicated the salon to be. Marjorie was surprised that the interview didn't include a tour of the beauty shop rather than a simple pointing out of the location.

Marjorie would take a peek on her own. She turned down a residential hallway. Perhaps she could get a glimpse of the typical clientele as she searched for the shop.

The institutional smells of lemon-scented cleanser and antiseptic tickled her nose. Marjorie sneezed. She'd likely get used to the scent, just as she had grown accustomed to the smell of bleach and ammonia in the orphanage.

In her opinion, there was little distinction between the nursing home and the orphanage. Both institutions housed people whom others could not—or would not—care for, while attempting to offer a "home sweet home" atmosphere. She suspected the assigned rooms, cafeteria trays, and common areas designed to encourage social interaction paled to the family dens and kitchen tables she'd seen in magazines or heard classmates describe. Indeed, the only difference between Hillhurst Nursing Home and Anderson Orphanage was the age of the occupants.

Marjorie's heels clicked on the floor. She grinned. The residents probably wouldn't hear her over the soap operas blaring from their rooms. Her eyes scanned the surroundings. Doors, most propped open, were set inside the concrete walls shaded to match wheat bread. Framed paintings provided the only source of bright color. Odd, some of the landscapes were beautifully done, while others were childlike replicas of those.

She examined an eye-catching painting of rolling hills covered in bluebonnets. The signature in the bottom right corner caught her eye. "DanielB." Formed one word and a small line extended from the "B" back toward the middle of the name. DanielB must be a resident here for his work to be displayed. Perhaps she'd meet him soon.

Curious whether the same artist painted all the refined pieces, she moved along the hallway, stopping in front of each one. Sure enough, Daniel B had made a name for himself here in Hillhurst. Did he know that his work was being copied in poor fashion?

Marjorie turned to leave met a male figure head-on. She startled. Yellowed strands of what once must have been white hair lay across a head speckled with age spots. At one time he may have towered over Marjorie, but his unruly spine forced him into a curved posture. He carried a book in his hand.

"Story day is Thursday. Is it story day?"

Marjorie smiled. "It's Thursday."

He extended the book toward her. "Will you read to me?"

Marjorie looked down the hall. Right about now she wouldn't mind running into personnel who could assist the man.

"Where is your room? I'll take you there."

"It's story day."

Apparently so.

She sensed someone coming up behind her. "Mr. Winkle, let's get you to your room." A young attendant wrinkled his brow at Marjorie. His reaction made her feel that she shouldn't be in the hallway with a resident.

"I was headed out when I came across him."

The elderly man shifted his focus to the attendant. "Story day is Thursday. Is it story day?" The two of them slipped into one of the rooms, and conversation faded. She took a deep breath and moved toward the door.

On to my next stop. No need to catch the city bus for that. The apartment complex Marjorie hoped to live in was within walking distance of Hillhurst. The few weeks of scanning newspapers for rooms to rent had not panned out. She'd been too late with her inquiry for both the ads she'd seen. The few remaining older orphans, like herself, had left weeks before and scattered to jobs and locations here and there across the county. With winning the scholarship for the local beauty school, Marjorie knew she needed to live in Hazel. She'd finally turned her thoughts toward the apartment complexes in town.

In addition to the ideal location, research had shown her the complex she was touring offered some furnished apartments. Now that she knew her salary, she could make an inquiry in person as though she were a respectable adult and not an overgrown orphan.

She strolled down the sidewalk, pausing to pick up a small flag, probably from the procession. Mr. Buckler's handsome face came to mind. Most likely a Mrs. Buckler existed, or at least a potential one, so she shouldn't think about his face. Besides, today's encounter would surely be their only one, especially since she would be moving from the orphanage and would no longer be near the school. She sucked in a breath. Had they encountered one another before and not realized it?

The complex appeared in front of her. Marjorie glanced at her watch. Ten minutes from the time she pushed through the nursing home door, she pulled open the door at the leasing office.

A young woman, perhaps her own age, looked up from her desk and displayed wide eyes and a hastened smile. A headband held back her blonde hair that flipped at the shoulders. She snuffed out her cigarette in a full ashtray. A short stack of saltine crackers lay next to the telephone.

Marjorie stopped short upon seeing the decor. Turquoise chairs shaped like a crescent moon were situated around white glossy tables displaying lava lamps. Yellow shagged carpet caught her eye. No hint of bleach or ammonia here, just the scent of nicotine in the air. Abstract art in bright colors hung on the white walls, creating a sense of noise and busyness, unlike the landscapes at Hillhurst that emanated peace.

"Hi. Can I help you?"

"I hope so. I'm here to inquire about a furnished one-bedroom apartment."

The woman lit another cigarette, then managed to smile and smoke simultaneously. "Fantastic. I have one unit left. It's the same floor plan as my own. I think you'll love it. I do." She opened a drawer and pulled out a miniature lava lamp key ring.

"Great!" *Seems adulthood is smiling on me.* "Let's take a look." *Perhaps I should verify the price before seeing the unit.*

Marjorie followed the leasing officer out the same doors she'd just entered.

"How much is the rent?"

"First things first. Fall in love, then pay the price. Isn't that the way of carefree living? Once you see this place, money will be of little concern." She let out a laugh.

Marjorie rolled her eyes. Little money was her concern.

The hostess stopped in front of a swimming pool and playground set on the common ground. She pointed, "The apartment is right over yonder, a short walk for an afternoon of sunbathing." Other than her bunk and a couple of drawers, everything at the orphanage was common. She looked forward to not sharing, though the thought of resting on a poolside lounge appealed to her. Perhaps this type of shared space wouldn't be too bad.

The leasing officer inserted a key into the white door numbered twenty-eight, then reached inside and flicked on the lights. She pushed the door wide, then spread her arms, letting ash fall onto the sidewalk. "Ta-da."

Marjorie stepped inside the unit and stared. Could this much space actually be hers to enjoy alone? She covered her mouth and stifled a yelp.

"I know it's ground level and someone will live a floor above you, and it's a bit cozy, but..."

"It's perfect." Marjorie moved through the space while catching the bits of information her hostess shared. The furniture was neat and not worn like that at the orphanage. The two-seat dinette situated by the brown refrigerator caught her eye with its metal legs and yellow top. Maybe she'd celebrate by baking a boxed cake in the brown oven she stared at.

She made her way to the bathroom and admired the one sink and one toilet. One sink—not a row of them and no row of stalls. And, her very own bathtub. Marjorie imagined herself getting ready without waiting her turn or trying to ignore a lump of toothpaste left in the sink by someone who'd primped before her.

She found herself back at the front door while her hostess continued her sales pitch. "Can't you just see a cute welcome mat here?" Marjorie nodded then stood beside the leasing agent as she locked the door.

"So, are you in love?"

"Well, I certainly could be. I suppose I need to know for sure what the rent is before I fall head over heels."

"I'll explain that back in the office. By the way, I'm Candace."

"I'm Marjorie."

Within two minutes, any hope faded. She couldn't afford the rent.

"Now, keep in mind, that price includes all your utilities and maintenance inside and outside."

"I understand, but it's more than I can pay."

"An unfurnished unit is less. And we have two available."

Marjorie saw images of herself sitting, sleeping, and eating on an empty floor. No way she could afford furniture.

"I appreciate your time, but I can't afford that either, right now."

The woman lit a cigarette and Marjorie noticed her brief look of pity before her abrupt retort. "Well, you won't find a better deal at the other complex in town."

That was the problem. Marjorie knew from research she wouldn't find a better deal because the other complex didn't offer a furnished unit. Deflated, she nodded her agreement and folded her hope into the price brochure, then handed it back to Candace.

Earlier she'd thought adulthood smiled on her because everything appeared to be going her way. She sensed now that adulthood still smiled, but with the gentle expression she imagined a parent would give a child who'd just figured out a truth. Life gives and withholds in measure.

Evening set in as Marjorie fidgeted with her watch. The bench at the bus stop felt cool since the warmer day temperatures had slipped away with the afternoon light. No matter how many scenarios she ran through her mind, Marjorie couldn't come up with another option for living life on her own. The orphanage would be under new management in a week, and all staff must be vacated. Miss Bords would be living in Arkansas in two days for her new job, so she couldn't stay with her.

She could embarrass herself and ask if Mr. Hurst had an empty room at the nursing home. Maybe she could rent it for a few days until she figured out something else. She snickered so she wouldn't cry. "Maybe I'll get hooked on a soap opera myself."

The bus pulled to a stop, and Marjorie dropped her coins into the pay slot and slid into the first empty aisle seat she noticed. She closed her eyes and rested her head against the seat back. She'd muster the courage to talk to Mr. Hurst before she was kicked out to the curb. She blew out a deep breath.

. . .

Daniel rubbed his aching neck as his stomach growled. He gaped at the pile of papers in front of him. Like rabbits, they seemed to multiply with each test he graded. He pulled a pencil from between his teeth, then tossed it and his red pen onto the coffee table. They landed on the last test he'd graded. Next to it lay twenty more needing his attention. He stood and stretched.

With four strides Daniel approached the refrigerator and opened the freezer door. Nope, despite the ice built up in his freezer, he hadn't overlooked an enchilada or Salisbury steak frozen dinner. A package of tater tots stared back at him, pleading to be freed from the frozen tundra. A quick look inside the refrigerator door, then the cupboard, revealed no ketchup. The tots were no longer a choice. Maybe he'd fry an egg. Another glance into the fridge mocked him. No eggs.

He grabbed his car keys from the wooden key holder his stepmother had hung by the front door. "No more misplacing your keys like your dad." She'd laughed as he'd eyed her gift on moving day. He had to admit, the contraption had spared him plenty of frustration. He did not miss the habit of hunting for his keys.

Lucy Buckler had been his mother longer than his real Mom had been before she died. Thinking of Lucy, he looked around his small house at several of his paintings which she had helped him hang. She had an eye for placement—and for talent. Like his birth mother before her, she had recognized Daniel's artistic ability and had fed it with supplies and art camp on more than one occasion.

It had also been her idea to hang some of his art in his classroom and at Hillhurst.

His stomach growled again, and Daniel trotted to his car. With his windows down and the popular "Twist" song blaring from the radio, he headed toward Taco Hacienda, twisting his torso to the beat. Just as the restaurant came into sight, the Funeral Lady came to mind.

Daniel needed to explore the idea that he'd been attracted to someone other than Candace. It wasn't that single women were nonexistent in his life since the failed relationship two years ago. Indeed, he encountered nice women at both school and church. Yet, their presence had never triggered the thought to move on that he'd sensed today.

Candace had done him wrong. So wrong. Yet, he'd found his heart a prisoner to her long after the betrayal. He rubbed his chin. Perhaps his heart fought for freedom.

Daniel pulled into a business parking lot and shut off the car. Away from the stacks of tests, with cool air hitting his face, he found his brain relaxed. His hunger could wait a moment longer. He rested his head against the seat back and turned down the radio.

Natives of Hazel, he and Candace had known one another since elementary school when he'd been struck by the wind blowing her long hair as she swung. At last, as they entered high school, he mustered the courage to ask her on a date. "The rest is history." He laughed, but the sound held no humor.

Daniel suspected Candace's change toward him began the first time he brought his new roommate, Conrad, home from college with him for the weekend to visit his family. Struck by a stomach bug, Daniel had spent most of the visit in bed. After work each evening, Candace had hung out with the family in his absence to make Conrad feel more at home. He had no reason at the time to suspect anything romantic stirred between them. He and Candace had already talked of marriage. Daniel just needed to make the proposal official. He'd graduate in May and suspected Candace would choose a summer wedding. A ring rested in his dresser drawer across from where he'd slept off his sickness.

Once he did propose, looking back, all talk between Candace and him had revolved around the wedding.

Not the relationship.

When Candace broke their engagement just before the rehearsal started, he hadn't seen it coming.

"Daniel, I can't marry you."

"You've got the jitters." He leaned in and kissed her cheek. She'd turned her head.

"I can't marry you because I've fallen in love with someone else." Daniel shuddered at the memory. The devastation had sent him out of town for days, praying to God and sorting through disappointment.

He'd managed a reply. "Who?"

"Conrad."

The best man. The college roommate. The jerk.

And two weeks later, news had reached him from Candace's family that she and Conrad had eloped and moved to Louisiana.

"Eloped!" Daniel shouted to the empty parking lot and banged the steering wheel. And dadgum, he never got back the ring.

Candace hadn't killed him, just deeply wounded him, and perhaps today healing had begun.

His stomach growled, and he headed toward the restaurant. The parking lot was packed when Daniel arrived. He excused himself through a crowd gathered inside the doorway awaiting a booth or a take-out order and made his way to the front register.

"I'd like a number ten to go."

"It'll be fifteen minutes. Want to wait at the bar?"

"No, thanks. I'll wait outside."

Daniel paid then made his way back to the car.

Grabbing the paperback copy of the novel in the passenger seat, he turned to the dog-eared page and began reading.

A presence at his car door made Daniel jump.

He turned his head to greet Martina Cortes, the Spanish teacher who taught across the hall, standing there with her husband.

"I heard you joined the dance committee." She, too, was a member.

"I begged to be accepted."

She responded with a deep laugh that didn't match her small frame.

Her husband joined in. "No doubt. What man wouldn't want to be on a junior high dance committee? Bummer." The owner of the local Hispanic market and meat house was a friendly man whose company Daniel enjoyed on the rare occasions they were together.

"Exactly." Daniel grinned. "Enjoy your supper."

The couple scurried to the restaurant door. Daniel checked his watch. Five more minutes before his order was ready. He could finish the chapter.

Daniel closed the book and headed inside. Soon he clutched a warm bag that released a pleasing aroma of spices. Glancing down to grab his keys from his pocket, he pushed to open the door with his shoulder, but someone held it open for him. He muttered a thanks.

"You're welcome, Danny."

Danny. Only one person had ever called him that.

Images of Candace dog-piled in his mind. Candace on the playground swing. Candace rolling up her rectangle pizza in the lunchroom; Candace nestled against him in the movie theater; Candace saying yes to his proposal.

Candace fleeing the scene of the wedding rehearsal.

This moment he must choose to form words, for none came naturally. Two syllables stumbled over his lips.

"Candace." He felt the warm sack of food slip from his fingers.

"It's good to see you, Danny."

Good to see him? That's what she had to offer? How about, "I'm so sorry I ruined your life," or "I'm so ashamed to face you."

"Don't call me Danny."

"Ok. Don't have a conniption fit. We should talk, Daniel."

Candace bent down and picked up the sack. He took advantage of her movement and high stepped it to his car.

She followed.

He leaned against the car door, with one hand on the handle. The other took the sack from her of its own free will. Afterall, a man had to eat.

"Did you hear what I said? We should talk."

"Maybe we should. Maybe we shouldn't." He shrugged.

She moved in, leaving inches between them. In another time he would have found the move inviting. He would have pulled his then fiancée to him and held her.

"Maybe you don't have anything to say, but I do."

"Apparently not those last two words."

"Danny—I mean, Daniel, that's not fair."

"There is no fair between us. Where's Conrad, your husband of two years?"

"He left me." Had she upturned his life too?

A sense of satisfaction came over him.

The feeling fed his appetite. He inhaled the scent of it. Tasted, and swallowed it. The concoction fed his need. His heart sent it to his veins and satisfaction pumped through him. He'd neither sought revenge nor wished it. But this was justice, and it tasted sweet.

God, forgive me. I shouldn't relish that she's hurting.

Tears rolled down her cheeks.

In contrast, something akin to sympathy enticed him. He pursed his lips against it, but the bittersweet elixir overtook his prior satisfaction. He knew what abandonment felt like. He wouldn't wish it on anyone. Not even the source of his own pain. The foundation of his character couldn't be denied, and with a grace that could only come from God, Daniel knew how he would respond. He could not deny that something shifted in him this morning at the procession, but for all he reckoned, Funeral Lady he noticed could have been an angel. Flesh and blood that he knew—had loved—stood before him. He'd offer her his compassion.

"I'm so sorry."

Her chin quivered. "No one deserves to be left." As she spoke, her voice shook. This may be as close to an apology as he'd get.

"No, they don't."

Awkwardness filled the inches between them. He needed words or he might hug her.

"Are you home visiting?" Healing? Starting over? On the prowl?

"I moved back a month ago."

His insides jolted.

"Oh."

"I'm managing that new apartment complex. Room and board come with the job." She grinned—a look that dreams are made of. He would have collapsed had the car door not held him up.

"Oh. Well, good for you. Look, I better split and get home before my food gets cold." He opened the car door, but before he could get in, her hand clasped his wrist.

"Can I meet you there?"

You mean, can you come to the house that I bought to be our home and let your perfume fill it?

A man should know how to respond when tempted.

3

This was her last time to work in the Anderson Orphanage office. She'd miss her boss, Miss Bords, but Marjorie reminded herself that the woman sitting at the desk behind her was not her mother, no matter how much she longed for one today. She was a superintendent. Indeed, Miss Bords had never birthed a child. Her mothering proved clinical and encumbered by red tape. Marjorie had never doubted that Miss Bords cared for those in her charge. A bit of protection here. A little admiration there. An occasional handling with utmost care. The orphans could just as well have been a treasured vase.

The practiced care was sufficient for daily orphanage life, but lacked during milestones when a parent would make a child feel special. Like graduating or getting a first job or glimpsing the most handsome man she'd ever seen.

Like a birthday. When a seven-year-old longed for a Cinderella cake with blue candles, but instead got the standard yellow with white frosting and candles she had to share with three other orphans. At least she could choose between chocolate or vanilla ice cream to go with her piece. That choice set the birthday children apart from the others at mealtime. And a new pair of socks and underclothing.

Princess cakes belonged to girls with mothers. Real mothers who breathed, laughed, and hugged. Not the mother of a young girl's imagination.

As Marjorie grew, so did her intolerance of the birthday ritual. Why celebrate the day that marked her as unwanted?

Yet, her imaginary mother wanted her "always and forever."

"Will you and Father get tired of me, Mother?"

"Never."

"Do you both still want me, Mother?"

"Always and forever."

Marjorie knew from her earliest recollections that she was an orphan, but when offered the opportunity at age twelve to understand why, she'd frozen in fear. Why would her mother choose to leave her here? She supposed that fear was misunderstood by others. She glanced at the file drawer of her desk. Inside lay a manila envelope containing her past.

"Marjorie, did you hear what I said?"

"No. My mind wandered." No, wondered. *Would I be better off opening the information and knowing?* She looked up to see Miss Bords eyeing her. The woman motioned for her to come sit in the chair beside her desk. Marjorie did.

Miss Bords offered her clinical smile. "Leaving the orphanage and moving into adulthood can be overwhelming for a life-timer."

"Life-timer? Please don't say that." The retort felt proper.

The middle-aged woman's high cheek bones turned a shade of pink. "I stand corrected. Your adult life is just beginning."

Marjorie's jaw dropped. Were Miss Bords' eyes watering?

"All these years, you have endeared yourself to me, the staff, and the children. Marjorie, over the years, only a few have nestled into my heart as you've managed to."

Marjorie felt her own eyes water. This was as close to "forever and always" as she'd ever been.

"Thank you, Miss Bords. I will miss you."

A broad grin spread across the administrator's face. "I personally picked out your goodbye gift, the shoes."

Marjorie inhaled. "They were perfect for my interview. Thank you."

"And I have another gift for you. From me personally—that is, not Miss Bords the superintendent." She pulled a small slim box from her desk drawer. "Open it."

Marjorie unwrapped the gift, then gasped. "It's lovely." She held up a delicate, gold-tone watch. Her heart swelled. "Thank you."

Marjorie moved to hug Miss Bords, but froze. The transformation had faded. Her clinical demeanor had returned.

"There is one more matter I want to discuss."

"Yes, ma'am?"

"You should open the envelope your mother left for you."

The fear kicked in. Every muscle tightened and bile rose in Marjorie's throat. Why had her parents never wanted her?

"Marjorie, the question why, which you have never asked me, would be answered."

She squared her shoulders. "I don't want to know."

"Your mother loved you."

Marjorie let out a soft gasp.

"You at least need to know that."

Marjorie fled the office.

• • •

The sobbing stopped. Once the door to Miss Bords' office shut, Marjorie had lost her composure and headed to the lavatory. She glanced in the bathroom mirror for a final inspection. The blotches were gone. She moistened her thumb then rubbed away a mascara smear. "All right." The huffed prompting echoed in the concrete and tile room. With the orphans in school, or work, the lavatory was vacant.

Marjorie moved to the sleeping quarters and grabbed her purse before making her way outdoors.

Your mother loved you.

The words spun through her mind, refusing to be ignored. Her head ached. Maybe she should rip open the envelope, and...*deal with my mother's sadness on top of my own at being left here?* She didn't want to know *why* she had been a burden her parents needed to hand over.

Marjorie shook the thoughts away. She didn't have the emotional stamina right now to face the truth.

Instead, she needed to focus on finding a place to live. She scurried out the front door of Anderson Orphanage.

Her eyes honed in on the junior high across the street. Was it just yesterday morning that she had been moved by the funeral procession and the handsome teacher? How life ebbed and flowed. Standing here twenty-four hours ago she'd felt mature and excited. This moment, the orphan morphed into a beggar. She would make her way to visit Mr. Hurst at the nursing home—not to accept a job, but to plead for room and board.

Marjorie rubbed her arms. She needed to concentrate on the good things life had given her—a scholarship and a job.

She crossed the street and sent a wave toward the school. "Hello, Mr. Buckler." Of course, she waved at no one. The school yard was empty. She smiled.

Within a half-hour, a secretary escorted her into Mr. Hurst's office. He stood as she entered. Marjorie sat in the same chair where she'd become employed. At Mr. Hurst's nod, the secretary took the other guest seat.

"I didn't expect to see you so soon, Miss. Mullins." The administrator sat, then leaned forward. "Is there an issue with the job?"

"No sir. I cannot wait to start work tomorrow. Thank you, again." Marjorie cleared her throat. No need wasting the man's time.

"I'm here because..."

Her confidence fled.

I'm homeless?

Stupid! Stupid! Stupid! I will not ask to live here.

Think!

"With the orphanage being sold and my job there ending, I have to find another place to live. I wondered if you knew a family who could use my help in exchange for minimal rent."

Though every muscle wanted to cower, Marjorie tightened her back and kept her eyes on the man. Might as well go down appearing strong.

Mr. Hurst tapped the desk with a pen before he leaned back. His chair squeaked and Marjorie jumped. "I'm afraid no one comes to mind." He looked at his secretary.

"I can't think of anyone either," she added to the conversation.

"I understand. Thank you for seeing me on short notice." She stood, hoping her humiliation and desperation weren't visible. At least she hadn't asked for a bed here.

"Hold on. Sit back down. Perhaps my wife could make some inquiries. She's very involved in the ladies' group at our church."

Marjorie dropped back into the chair. "You would ask her to do that, sir?"

"Yes. It's no problem. But, it's also no promise."

"I understand. Thank you."

"Miss Mullins, who knows what the Good Lord might have in store."

The Good Lord? Marjorie grimaced. Not once had she acknowledged God in her recent circumstances, good or bad. Her mind flashed back to Miss Carter, the Baptist preacher's sister who came and taught the orphans Sunday School every Sunday afternoon. Marjorie attended each week and learned all the memory verses. Yes, she'd even prayed for Jesus to forgive her sins.

How long had it been since she'd opened her Bible and read a scripture? Miss Carter's words stretched and yawned from their long rest. "God is a Father who will always love you." Somewhere between adolescence and adulthood, Marjorie had tucked those words into bed and bid them a long, good night. Perhaps she would give God more attention in the future.

She stood. "Thank you, Mr. Hurst."

Marjorie left the office still homeless, but not quite hopeless.

• • •

A voice pulled Daniel's mind from the fog. "Allied Forces."

"Mr. Buckler?" The same voice with an inquisitive tone.

"Pardon me?"

"The answer to your question, Mr. Buckler. It's Allied Forces."

The teacher jostled his thoughts and gave a hurried glance at his surroundings. The classroom on a Friday afternoon. Not his house late last night.

He'd just asked the students a question. "Correct, Rusty."

Snickering meandered through the desks. "Mr. Buckler has a hangover." The snickers exploded into laughter.

One had to drink to have a hangover, and Daniel was a tee-totaler. But if indiscretion caused a hangover, then Curtis hadn't misspoken. He'd simply earned himself a reprimand.

"Curtis, stand up." The boy stood and swayed. "Yesss shirrr."

The classroom grew silent. Even by eighth-grade standards, Curtis had gone too far.

"You disrespected me."

"All I did was tell the truth."

Daniel didn't flinch.

"Class, I'll be accompanying Curtis to the principal's office. I've listed six questions on the board. Answer them as though you were an Allied soldier. Due at the end of the period."

Daniel moved to stand next to Curtis and motioned him to follow. The boy's expression sobered.

As they rounded the corner, Mrs. Cortes met them from the opposite direction and stopped.

"Mr. Buckler, here's your planning notebook for the dance. I was just bringing it to you for the Tuesday meeting."

Did she think he and Curtis were on a friendly walk about?

"Thanks." Daniel took the binder. "I'll look through it later." He indicated Curtis with his eyes.

"Oh." Mrs. Cortes' eyes widened. "Pardon the interruption." She scurried away.

"This dance will be boring," Curtis mock whispered.

Daniel kept quiet and held back a grin. On this topic, he and Curtis saw eye to eye.

. . .

Daniel rubbed his whiskers, embarrassed to face his reflection in the mirror. He considered himself a level-headed, Godly man, but allowing Candace into his house was a mistake. He should have at least stepped onto his front porch when she showed up. He'd fallen so easily into physical attraction with her nearby. Was that all he'd ever had for her? He hoped he was a better man than that.

No, what he'd once felt for Candace had been as strong internally as it was physically.

He'd spent the school day dwelling on the evening. No doubt the students noticed. Curtis' hangover comment proved that point.

When he'd arrived back home after school, the smell of spices, perfume, and hints of cigarettes lingered, and he'd flung open the windows. He'd been shocked last night to learn that Candace took up smoking, and that she'd been so forward with him. She seemed anything but the innocent, modest girl he'd known. Running a comb through his hair and brushing his teeth, he huffed. His house was the last place he wanted to be tonight.

He closed his windows in spite of the odors and headed to his parents' house for Fall Friday Chili Night. Daniel hadn't participated in the family tradition for a couple of weeks, and his stepmother would likely be thrilled to have him. His dad would likely notice his demeanor and find a way to talk through the matter weighing on Daniel's mind.

He'd been honorable with Candace last night when her intentions were made clear by her inviting actions. How easily she'd shrugged off the "glitch," her word for the broken engagement, in their relationship and offered to move forward, at least physically. He shook away the image as he put his key into the ignition.

Rainclouds darkened the sky. Pretty much summed up his mood. The conclusion of the conversation played on his mind.

"Conrad chose to leave me. We won't get back together. I'll be a divorcée. Do you think God will forgive that?" She'd reached into her purse and pulled out cigarettes.

"Don't."

She'd winked and threw the pack on the table. "You should try it. You may like it. Might break your nasty habit of chewing pencils."

"Talk to Conrad. He may regret leaving you."

She nodded her head back and forth.

"I made a poor choice to walk away from you. I love you, Danny." She'd slid next to him and fingered the hair at his neck while pulling his mouth to hers and kissed him. Her other hand rested on his chest.

The man in him responded.

He wanted the affection of a woman.

But not with her.

That longing was reserved for a wife who loved him.

The gentleman in him pushed her away.

"I want you back, Daniel. I never stopped loving you."

"Actions speak louder than words." Good grief. He sounded like one of his students issuing a "nana nana boo boo."

She remained seated and stared at him as though challenging his will.

"I don't love you anymore, Candace." A moment of truth. His affection had suffered a slow and painful death. He hadn't recognized love's demise until he spoke the words aloud. "And I choose not to try again."

Angry, Candace stalked to the door without a fight. Proof she didn't love him. Proof she hated rejection.

Daniel parked the car outside his family home and squeezed his eyes closed against the memory. Once inside, he joined the chatter at the dining room table.

"So, I got appointed to the dance committee at school."

"The dance. How dreamy." His half-sister, Tali, mimicked a swoon. Her sixth-grade self had quite a romantic bent.

Daniel laughed. "If you can call hanging streamers and toting boxes of decorations dreamy."

She kicked him under the table. "Party pooper. I can't wait for my turn to attend the dance."

Daniel grinned. Tali would be in junior high next year. The halls would sparkle with her presence. At least she had to wait until eighth grade to attend the dance. His parents would have their work cut out for them keeping hormonal boys at bay. Daniel knew far too much about the habits of junior high males. His sense of protection growled within him.

Daniel appreciated every bite of his stepmother's meal, but when she offered dessert, he declined. The burden he carried unsettled him. He made his way to the front porch, and as though he were a mind-reader, his father followed him.

A trim man with broad shoulders, Leland Buckler shared facial features with his son. Daniel didn't consider himself vain, but he knew his father was a handsome man and that they looked alike. His father's reputation was accurate—he had integrity and was loyal to his family and God. And a good lawyer.

Those two traits and good looks were where their similarities ended. Daniel's talents and mellow temperament were all from his mother. She too had been a teacher. If given the ability, his mother would have carried every burden of those she loved. And, though she lacked her son's talent, the woman painted to relax. He relished boyhood memories of sitting at her feet mimicking her paintbrush strokes.

Daniel hunched on the top step while his father leaned against a pole, sheltered beneath the roof. The man rolled a toothpick in his mouth. Rain pattered from the gutter on the porch corner. A cool mist dampened Daniel's hair.

"Son, got something on your mind?"

"You noticed?"

"That wrinkled brow is a giveaway. And turning down dessert."

"I found myself in a bind last night. It was a mistake."

"We all do from time to time. Did you learn from it?"

"Yes. I learned that I'm not in love with Candace anymore."

He watched his father suppress a smile. A trick of his trade.

"I saw that tamed look, Dad." Daniel grinned. He'd felt pain when Candace betrayed him. His parents had felt anger. She'd fallen from their graces with a thud. Their parental support comforted him and cushioned his humiliation.

"Sorry, Son. I let go of my anger a while back. But I won't deny I'm relieved by your words." He shifted to lean against the porch rail. "There's a mistake in there somehow?"

"She's back in town." Not an answer, but the path to it.

"What?"

"Conrad left her."

"Well, I'll be." Daniel knew the expression revealed his dad's shock. The man could usually find his words.

"I let her in my house last night."

"The bad decision?"

Daniel nodded. "Her motive wasn't good, and I pushed her away."

His Dad blew out a breath.

Daniel explained the events of the previous night.

"Maybe you can move on now."

"Maybe."

And maybe he'd see the Funeral Lady again in a crowd.

Yeah. And maybe he would win a million dollars too.

4

Marjorie sneezed and almost dropped the damp, used towels. She'd sucked in a breath just as Gordon Dixon, the male beautician, sprayed his client's hair. The hunched and frail woman sitting in his salon chair looked as though she could use a booster seat.

She smiled. This was a good Saturday. Midway through her first day at the shop, and she'd already watched the man pamper three clients. His gestures were smooth, but not near as smooth as his voice. Not in a sensual way, but in a calming, reassuring way. A movie star wouldn't have received better treatment than the elderly ladies whose hair he'd washed and styled. All three women had left the shop smiling as they turned toward the social hall.

Best she could guess, the man neared forty. His left hand sported a gold band, and his work area displayed a photo of a woman and children. Her observations and his brief nice-to-meet-you this morning before Valene gave her a tour were all she knew about Gordon, but she liked him.

She used her foot and pushed open the laundry room door. The hum of the dryer and swish of the washer testified to her hard work. A sense of satisfaction came over her. She dropped the wet towels into a plastic hamper and grabbed the broom and dustpan from the hook on the opposite wall.

The compact room also boasted a folding table with two chairs, coat hooks, and a small counter that held an electric percolator and some snacks. A refrigerator took up its own corner adjacent to the door.

The small shop contained three stations, two bowls, and two hair dryers. Three waiting chairs were arranged into a small corner space with a table. Magazines were fanned across it. A rolling manicure cart and seat were nestled between the two hair dryers. The laundry room sat next to another room that housed inventory and a small desk. The sign on that door read "Office." Only one exterior entrance to the salon existed for the staff. Residents entered from an interior door off the social hall in the nursing home. It had been propped open all morning, and Marjorie caught glimpses of residents, staff, and perhaps guests moving to and fro. The aroma of shampoo and hair spray hid the institutional scents.

Marjorie swept the cuttings from Gordon's last customer while he dropped the combs into the disinfectant solution. She noted three pictures on the wall opposite the dryers. Each displayed a different young woman with a different modern hairstyle. The angle of the picture highlighted the hair. No doubt the women were models. And no doubt, the clients that entered this shop would never resemble the women in the pictures—at least not anymore, courtesy of age.

"Gordon, why does the shop display those pictures instead of ones with older women?" Her cheeks warmed. She wished she hadn't asked the question. An awkward silence as she swept would have been more tolerable than her awkward inquiry.

The man turned his head toward her with no hint of irritation on his face. He gestured toward the picture. "It doesn't matter that our clients cannot look like those women. What matters is if they feel that beautiful when they leave our shop." He winked. "Beauty school won't teach you that lesson. It comes from experience."

Marjorie stilled, but her heart beat faster. He'd pegged her. She had always enjoyed making people feel special. The longing to do so in this shop skittered through her alive and well.

"I've watched you do that very thing all morning. I hope to follow your example."

"Thank you. Valene told me you won the scholarship. Congratulations."

"Thanks. I'm excited to start Tuesday." She resumed sweeping as Gordon moved toward the laundry room.

Just then, Valene emerged from the office where she'd been holed up most of the morning. "Well, the books are balanced and the orders are placed. Just in time for my appointment." She tugged at a wrinkle in the skirt of her white uniform. "You two get to know one another a bit?"

Gordon halted in the laundry room doorway. "Just a bit. My happy, chatty ladies kept me occupied."

Marjorie laughed at his accurate description.

Valene grinned. "Well, folks, the tone in here is about to change with my next client."

Gordon raised his eyebrows and smiled at Valene. Clueless of the obvious understanding between them, Marjorie remained quiet.

Valene pulled a plastic drape from the bottom drawer of her station and shook it out. "Marjorie, have you stayed busy?"

"Yes, very."

"Any questions for me?"

"Not that I can think of. Well, you will tell me if I don't do something the right way? Or overlook something?"

"Of course. It looks clean in here. I think you're getting the hang of things. Once I get my next customer shampooed and you gather the towels, take your lunch break."

"Sure."

A figure appeared in the interior doorway. Unlike the earlier clientele Marjorie had seen this morning, the lady entering the shop stood tall and broad. Pale foundation and two spots of rouge covered her round face. She boasted a green eyeshadow that fought with her green eyes. Yet, her defining feature was the auburn hair. She cleared her throat.

"I hope you are ready for me, Valene. I'm punctual as usual"

"Good morning, Wanda. Have a seat. I'm ready. We do the same routine every week. I'm always ready." Valene swiveled the salon chair so the client could slide in comfortably. Just as Wanda eased into the chair, her eyes locked with Marjorie's gaze. Marjorie felt her skin tighten as the woman stared at her.

"Who's that?" The question was addressed to Valene.

"This is Marjorie. She begins beauty school Tuesday and will work here Saturday afternoons and Mondays."

"Well, she can keep her hands out of my hair."

Marjorie coughed—the combination of a laugh and a gasp.

Valene patted the woman's shoulder. "Now, Wanda, don't you worry about a thing."

Her boss turned toward her and smiled. "Marjorie, on second thought, why don't you go ahead and take your lunch break? You can tidy up later."

Marjorie took the hint. Appreciated it. Obeyed it. With a quick step into the laundry room, she grabbed her lunch from the refrigerator and sat across the table from Gordon.

"You met Wanda." He smiled.

"More like encountered her."

"Don't let her fool ya. She's soft inside."

"Deep inside?"

Gordon laughed, then picked up a cookie resting on a square of tin foil. "Like this sandwich cookie. Thin layers of hard protecting the sweet." He tossed the entire cookie into his mouth. "My kids' favorite," he mumbled.

"I'll try to remember that about her." Marjorie released a smile, then pulled her bologna sandwich from her lunch bag.

Both of them turned as Mr. Hurst entered the cramped room. "Just stopped by to welcome you, Miss Mullins."

"Thank you."

"My wife made some calls last night, but nothing came of them. Keep your chin up. The word is out."

She wanted to crawl beneath the table. "I understand. Thank you so much. And thank your wife for me." The man acknowledged Gordon then turned back into the salon. Marjorie overheard Mr. Hurst tell Wanda he'd attended the funeral procession. Perhaps she valued patriotism. The rest of the conversation muffled when Gordon spoke up.

"You know Mrs. Hurst?"

Marjorie couldn't t blame the man for asking. Both polite conversation and curiosity could deem the inquiry normal. Might as well get her situation out in the open.

"No. I've never met her. Mr. Hurst knows I need a place to live. His wife made some calls to try and help."

Valene's perfume announced her presence. Marjorie inhaled the warm, heavy, but pleasing scent. She directed her attention to Marjorie. "I overheard that. It never occurred to me that you'd have to move. You're welcome on my couch for a few days."

Marjorie's insides flipped and flopped.

"That's so nice, but I couldn't impose."

"I wouldn't offer if I didn't mean it."

A silence slipped in. She longed to be a mature, young adult, not immature and needy, but she couldn't sleep on maturity.

"Then, yes, I'd be grateful. Just for a few days."

"Exactly." Valene's kindness had a practical side.

Gordon interjected. "I can help move your things."

"Thanks, but all my belongings from the orphanage will fit in a couple of boxes."

Understanding moved across his face.

"We'll work out the details. Meanwhile," Valene motioned toward Wanda, who sat in the styling chair with her hair wrapped in a towel, "our client insists on seeing you, if you don't mind."

"Don't keep her waiting." Gordon pointed to another cookie and chuckled.

Within seconds, she forced a smile and stood beside the salon chair. Valene combed Wanda's wet hair and smiled. "Creme rinse works wonders"

"Do you know what a creme rinse is, young lady?" Wanda's question landed on Marjorie's shoulder.

"Yes. It untangles hair after a shampoo."

"And what is a bluing rinse?"

"Uh, it gives yellowed hair a white luster." *I hope.*

From the corner of her eye, Marjorie noticed Valene's smile.

"Humph." Wanda didn't smile. "Tell me, Marjorie. Why do you deserve this scholarship?"

I'm not obligated to answer that question.

Marjorie glanced at Valene, whose nod indicated to humor the client.

"Because I want to help people feel special, and I have a talent for doing hair."

"Your parents can't afford to pay for your education?"

How rude. Another glance at Valene revealed her boss's blush. Valene likely hadn't anticipated such a personal question. The client must be rather cantankerous, and for the sake of her new boss, she answered.

"No. That is, I don't have parents."

'They died?"

"I don't know. I grew up in the orphanage." Marjorie hoped the woman felt satisfied now that she had shared her humiliating heritage.

Wanda's expression softened briefly, then hardened. "Family is important."

Well, yes, but Marjorie had no choice in the matter. Her family dwelt in a sealed envelope. She stifled her agitation. "Yes ma'am, I agree. Even though I don't have one."

"Well, let's hope you are self-motivated and don't waste the scholarship."

Marjorie watched as Valene stopped combing out Wanda's hair and placed her hands on the woman's shoulders. "I'm sure Marjorie will do a fantastic job in school. I wouldn't have hired her if I thought differently."

Marjorie wanted to hug her boss.

"Ma'am, the scholarship and this job are the best things that've ever happened in my life. I'll do my best at both." Marjorie piddled with her watch band.

Valene dismissed her to finish lunch. With sheer willpower, she smiled at Wanda before turning away. "Have a good afternoon."

· · ·

After the encounter with Wanda, the rest of the day proved to be pleasant. Goodbyes being said, Marjorie grabbed her purse and scurried out the back door. She glanced at her watch. The bus wasn't due for another half-hour. She'd have time to relax and consider the arrangements she and Valene had made about her move.

Being an adult hadn't removed the stigma of having no one to lean on. Valene was generous. She was kind. But she was her boss, and Marjorie would continue to be a guest in someone else's home. She'd spent a lifetime being a temporary resident living with a calculated deadline.

Gravel popped beneath her feet as she moved through the parking lot. That sound always relaxed her. She noted a figure bent over the open trunk of a red convertible. Marjorie paused to observe. Easels were tucked under one arm. A black case splotched with color rested against a tire. Were those blank canvases leaning against the other tire?

The figure stood upright, and Marjorie gasped. *Mr. Buckler.*

He gripped a pencil between his teeth. A more casual, humorous image than his suit and tie.

Her stomach fluttered. She felt silly to think he might remember her.

He yanked the pencil from his mouth. "Hi."

"Hi."

He cleared his throat. "You're the woman my student ran into, right?"

Yes! I'm her, Mr. Buckler. You remembered what I look like.

"I sure am." She glanced at his left hand. No wedding band, but that didn't mean no girlfriend or fiancé.

He stepped closer. "Are you sure you're okay? I should have checked on you more intentionally. Rusty isn't a small kid, but he's a good one."

"Oh, I'm fine. I'm Marjorie." She held out her hand. Oops. She reckoned the man should do this first?

He tossed the pencil into the trunk and swiped a palm on his jeans before reaching for her hand. In quick motion, he withdrew the offer. As quickly as one might plunge a knife into a victim's heart. Marjorie felt the heat in her face.

"Sorry. My hands are kind of dirty. I'm Daniel."

Mr. Buckler. Daniel Buckler. DanielB? The easels and canvases implied such.

"It's good to meet you. Are you by chance, the artist, DanielB?"

"I am. You've seen my work." He smiled.

"Yes, in the halls here. I think your paintings are lovely." *Lovely? Not a guy word.* "I enjoy the scenes and colors."

He blushed. "Thanks. I teach afternoon painting classes for the residents a couple times a week."

She opened her mouth to respond, yet his words continued. "I've never seen you here before."

"You haven't?"

"No. I think I would remember."

"I'm kidding. I just started working at the shop today."

"Cool. Hey, are you hungry? I am gonna grab a burger right quick. That is, if I'm not imposing on another man's lady."

What a predicament. No car. No home. If she said yes, then what? Her situation couldn't stay hidden and would impose on him. He'd offer to drive her home.

"No, you're not, and thank you. But I can't today." The rejection scraped her throat on its way out. She wrapped it in a soft smile and hoped it landed gently on his ears.

His blush indicated otherwise.

She blamed her parents. Their "I can't" had forced hers.

5

"Oh, no!" Marjorie's hand grew clammy against the plastic handle of her worn suitcase.

She hoped Valene didn't hear the exclamation. When she noticed two white, long-haired felines stretched across Valene's red couch, the words escaped as a memory leapt forward. Five-year-old Marjorie had rescued a stray cat from the orphanage playground and moments later found herself straining to breathe. Cats took her breath away—literally. Since then, she'd avoided any potential encounters with the creatures.

Why didn't I ask Valene if she owned a cat?

Because I was desperate to find a place to live.

She composed herself and took in the rest of the view. Valene had style. The red couch was the focal point of a room with brown paneling, a braided rug, and two yellow chairs with skinny legs. A coffee table that complemented the paneling rested in front of the couch. In view of the two chairs stood a television. Multi-colored wicker light shades hung from the ceiling. A dinette set with four red chairs sat to the left, lending access to the kitchen and a good view of the television. Plants added splashes of green across the view. The room felt tight, but bright.

"This is lovely."

Her boss closed the door behind them then moved to open multi-colored curtains, revealing sliding doors and a cement patio. "Thank you. Let me show you around. Leave your suitcase here."

Marjorie followed her boss through the small home, noting its tidiness. She stopped short at the sight of a second, fully furnished bedroom. Valene had offered her the couch. Did someone else live here?

Her hostess entered the hall bathroom and opened the medicine cabinet. "I cleared some space for you on the top shelf." Men's shaving cream and a razor rested below the empty shelf. Beside that lay a tube of used toothpaste and a toothbrush. A bottle of aspirin and men's cologne rested on the bottom shelf.

Uneasiness edged its way up Marjorie's spine. She'd certainly shared a bathroom, but never with a man.

"Oh, if you don't mind sharing space with my brother, you can sleep in the extra bedroom instead of the couch."

"Sharing space?"

Valene guffawed. "I guess that sounded awkward."

"Yes."

Valene brushed her hand over Marjorie's shoulder.

"I'm sorry. My brother crashes here from time to time, so I consider that room his. But I've asked him not to sleep over while you're here for the week."

"Whew. Yes, I'd be happy to use his space."

"Use. That sounds a lot better than share." Valene grinned while heading into the bedroom. "Here, the bottom half of the chest of drawers is empty. Is this enough room?"

"Plenty. I really appreciate your hospitality and kindness."

"You're welcome." Her boss tapped the bed. "Sheets are clean. I'd like you to make the bed each morning before you leave."

"Absolutely." She bit her tongue against adding "with military corners" as she'd been taught at the orphanage.

One white feline eased by Valene's feet. She gathered the pet into her arms and began stroking it. Marjorie stifled a sneeze as a thought nagged her. This was not home and she didn't belong here.

"Well, why don't you grab your suitcase and get settled? I have goulash left over from last night. We'll eat in about fifteen minutes."

"Sounds good."

Marjorie followed her hostess down the narrow hall back toward the living room.

Marjorie grasped her worn suitcase from the donations room at the orphanage and placed it on the bed.

Her head ached. This Sunday had not been a day of rest, and saying goodbye at the orphanage had squeezed her heart tighter than she'd anticipated.

She sneezed. And sneezed again.

The cats!

Her eyes itched, but her throat hadn't closed. At least for now, she could breathe in more ways than one.

"Achoo."

. . .

"The goulash is an old family recipe." Valene tapped the serving spoon against the edge of the orange bowl after serving herself seconds. Sitting at a table in this home, using Melmac plates with a funky turquoise design on them had set Marjorie's nerves at ease.

The goulash even smelled better coming from a homey kitchen than it had as a staple at the orphanage.

"Thanks for supper. I can do the dishes." Marjorie picked up her plate and rose from the table, just as another sneeze announced itself.

"Bless you. Are you getting sick? You kind of sound stopped up."

Marjorie felt her supper stir. She wrestled her instinct to lie when feeling caught.

"Well. I'm allergic to cats." The words tumbled over one another.

Dread came over her as Valene stiffened and her face reddened. "I didn't think to tell you I had cats."

"I didn't think to ask." *Because I was desperate.* "I'm embarrassed. I can find somewhere else to stay."

Valene crumpled her paper napkin onto the table.

"No, unless you want to. We'll manage for a few days if you can."

"I figured I can hang out in the bedroom most of the time."

"Well, my sweethearts can stay in my room during the evenings. They sleep there anyway."

No matter the solution, Marjorie realized cat hair would be all over the house. She'd have to make the best of the situation.

Valene scooped the cats from a yellow chair and hastened down the hall. Marjorie couldn't read her mood. She did not desire awkwardness on the personal level with her new boss. Displacing both Valene's pets and her brother felt intrusive.

She cleared the table, then they managed the dishes together. The chatter of getting acquainted eased Marjorie's tension. She decided to ask about Wanda. Time and timidity had kept her from asking about Valene's brash client. Now Time was at hand, and Timidity was not.

"I'm so curious. Why was your client, Wanda, testing me to see what I knew about rinses and stuff?" Marjorie wanted to add, "And why did you set me up to be questioned?" She resisted.

Valene chuckled. "Wanda is old and meddlesome, for sure. But you two share a passion."

"I can't imagine one thing we have in common."

Valene slid a plate into the cabinet. "Wait here." She smiled. "I'll be right back to explain."

Marjorie dried the silverware and put it away as Valene returned carrying a book.

Recognition registered and Marjorie's mouth popped open. "That's a cosmetology textbook."

Valene handed it to her and grinned. "It's mine. Open it to the front flap and read."

Marjorie opened the front cover. "Valene, in all my years as a teacher, you are my prize pupil. You bring out the best in your clients. Keep up the good work. Love, Wanda."

The words settled into her mind. "Wanda was your beauty school teacher?"

"Yes." Valene sat down in her seat.

"So, you're saying hair is our shared passion?"

"Yep. Wanda and me stayed in touch after I completed school here in Hazel. I worked in a Dallas salon for several years, and when I learned she was moved into Hillhurst, I left Dallas and opened up The Wright Do. Wanda is family to me. Not by blood, but by heart."

"What a sweet story. I just realized that you learned at the same school I'm attending."

"That's right."

"So, that explains Wanda's interest in the scholarship."

"Mostly." Valene sipped her tea.

"Mostly?"

"She's the one who started the scholarship, though now the administration selects the recipient."

"I'm flabbergasted."

Her boss's laughter filled the air.

"So, don't take her comments personally. Just realize the scholarship is personal to her."

"Gordon says she's like a sandwich cookie—hard on the outside, but soft and sweet inside."

"Leave it to Gordon to describe someone as food, but that's a good description. Wanda taught him too. Gordon and I worked together in Dallas for a while."

"So, he came to Hazel when you opened The Wright Do?"

"No. By chance, he'd moved to Hazel about five years before I opened shop. He was my first hire."

Valene gasped and looked at her watch, then stood in haste, snipping the conversation. Marjorie sucked in a breath, uncertain what had just happened.

Valene opened the refrigerator freezer and offered her an ice cream sandwich. "But now, it's time for television. It's a Sunday night tradition. I eat an ice cream sandwich while I watch that cowboy Brett" She winked. "My brother teases that my dream is to become Mrs. Maverick."

Marjorie laughed. "He is handsome." *Why isn't Valene married?* She kept the question to herself. Maybe one day she'd know her story,

The television show theme song began, but Marjorie's thoughts moved to Daniel Buckler, not a fictional character. Had she freaked him out yesterday when she declined lunch? Was disappointment nagging him like it was nagging her? *He was probably just being kind when he offered.* The soothing tactic cowered each time she recalled his words, "I think I would remember."

She couldn't wait to start school Tuesday, yet she was curious to discover if she might run into Daniel at Hillhurst tomorrow, though he never said what days, other than obviously Saturday, he worked there. If he asked her to grab a burger again, she wouldn't hesitate.

Sitting on the couch gave Marjorie a different angle, and she spotted a framed photograph on a wall shelf. While a commercial ran, she stood to go look at it. Four people smiled at the camera. One was obviously Valene.

"Is this your family?"

"Yeah. My parents and my younger brother, from a few years ago."

Her brother was familiar.

Good grief. He resembled the intern who'd encountered her in the Hillhurst hallway.

"Do they live here?"

"They live in Waxee. My brother is an intern at Hillhurst and crashes here a lot to avoid driving back and forth after work."

"Oh. What's his name?"

"Stewart. You may recognize him from elementary school. My family lived here for a bit, in the same district as the orphanage. I figure he went to the elementary school about the same time you did."

She didn't recognize him from school, just from the Hillhurst. But his image conjured a strange feeling she couldn't peg

"I was so shy and timid when I was I school. Stewart Wright. Nothing rings a bell."

Just a weird feeling.

. . .

Daniel thumbed the pages of his teacher textbook to determine how much of the WWII unit he had left to teach. There was so much more to history than he taught at the eighth-grade level. Yet, he enjoyed teaching impressionable teens the "bullet points," as he called them. The challenge of capturing their interest then seeing them engage fulfilled him.

He glanced at the clock in his kitchen and sighed. He'd stayed longer at his parents after church today than he usually did. He'd needed the time to settle his nerves. Throughout Sunday School and the service, he'd felt on edge, afraid Candace would walk in announcing her return to Hazel. When she hadn't appeared, he'd conjured images of her stopping by his house. So, he'd hid at his parents' home until the evening. His heart twinged. "Lord, forgive me for my sarcasm. I know Candace is hurting. Trust me, I know. Help her."

He rose from his couch and patted his midsection. He'd eaten too much of his stepmother's Sunday pot roast. He should've accepted the roast sandwich she offered for supper rather than filling another plate as full as the lunch one. He stretched. It would be his last decent meal until next weekend when he'd visit them again.

A walk down his street might invigorate him. Daniel closed his lesson plan book and headed out. A warm breeze welcomed him.

Street lights sent a soft glow onto the sidewalk. One could see for miles in the flat geography of Hazel, Texas. Though he didn't don a cowboy hat and boots, Daniel felt proud to be a Texan.

He enjoyed his small neighborhood. Most of the residents were older couples whose grandchildren occasionally filled the streets with noise. Otherwise, the dated subdivision remained still and quiet. Men waved at one another as they tended their yards. Women chatted across flower beds. If it weren't for his step-mother and Tali, who loved to garden and insisted on caring for his flower beds, his would be an eyesore. Summer evenings found most residents sitting in lawn chairs on the driveways sipping beverages or at card tables playing poker and canasta. Daniel played neither and tended to avoid the driveway ritual.

How fortunate he'd been to snag such a good deal on his house. Not to mention the fact that his dad gave him his own convertible when he graduated college. Teachers didn't go into the profession to make money.

Daniel shook his head side to side recalling what a novelty he'd been when he'd first moved in two years ago. The neighborhood women had fed him with cakes and casseroles, certain the young bachelor didn't know his way around a kitchen. He still didn't, and once his newness wore off and his future wife walked away, he became a connoisseur of frozen dinners. At least a sweet lady at Hillhurst baked him the occasional pie.

His mind wondered to Marjorie. Sure, he hadn't asked a woman to spend time with him since he'd been jilted, but he had no idea how rusty his skills had become. He could count on less than ten fingers the sentences shared between them before he blurted his invitation to lunch.

He should count his lucky stars she hadn't yelled for help. He'd embarrassed both of them no doubt.

But he had no reason to think she'd lied when she answered "I can't." Perhaps she could another time. He'd ask again without hesitation. He'd be at Hillhurst tomorrow to teach his art class. Would she?

Had Marjorie caught the truth that slipped from his mouth? "I think I would remember." If so, had she thought he was just dropping her a line? It likely sounded that way, though he felt he'd spoken the truth.

Perhaps God was making it easy for him to move forward and trust his heart with someone new. He'd placed the woman in his path at the procession. Then He'd even dropped her smack dab in front of him in the parking lot. Maybe both his healing and resilience were being proved. He wanted to get to know her.

Daniel turned at the corner and headed back toward his house, lulled by the bullfrogs bellowing in the nearby pond. He whistled. Perhaps his heart was ready to be captured again without history repeating itself. He should take that risk. Marjorie had a smile that turned him into a goofy eighth-grader. Maybe he'd stray from painting landscapes and try his hand at capturing that smile.

His laughter blended with the bullfrogs' song until the shrill ring of his telephone startled him. He bustled inside.

"Hel-oh. Daniel here."

If Daniel were a cussing man, he'd have done so now. Instead, he rested his fist against the wall to steady himself.

"Listen, Conrad. Man, I don't need or want to know anymore what happened between you and Candace back then."

Conrad kept talking. Daniel let out a breath. "And I don't need to know what happened between you now. But maybe you should take her back." The voice on the other end went silent before the receiver clicked. Daniel sucked in a breath.

Conrad had hung up.

Daniel hung up his own telephone then proceeded to pace his driveway. The last thing he wanted was to be mixed up in Conrad and Candace's mess. He wished Candace had never come back to Hazel.

Why had the past come to visit—or worse—come to stay?

6

Marjorie tapped her foot to the big band tune playing softly on the radio. Valene knew her customers felt at home with the tunes of the '40s more than the popular rock and roll hits of the day.

Marjorie glanced over the shampoo bowl as she wiped it down and noticed Gordon pull a small jar from his pants pocket. He handed it to the petite, elderly lady shuffling into the salon. The wide entry from the hallway would fit three of her tiny frame. Her thin structure and white hair resembled a cotton swab. Marjorie did a double take. The woman had a yellow-checked kitchen apron tied around her waist. What type of woman wore a kitchen apron to get her hair done?

Intrigued and humored, Marjorie folded the wash cloth she was using at the shampoo bowl, stuffed it in her uniform pocket, and eased closer to the hair station. The brass and snare drums gave way to a mellow crooner while the hair dryer whirred in rhythm. Marjorie's curiosity evolved into pleasure as the apron lady swayed and mouthed the words of the song. Perhaps the woman had drifted into a romantic memory, if only for a second.

Marjorie had found an unexpected treasure in her short time at the shop. The residents were delightful, interesting, and had a lifetime of stories to tell. Except Wanda. Surely, she had stories of her own, but did she ever show her personal side? Marjorie's skin prickled as she recalled the woman's tone.

Despite Wanda, Marjorie found herself struck with the dimension the older generation added to her life. She'd had no experience with grandparents. A worn truth stood front and center in her mind. The Anderson Orphanage, the only place she'd lived, was a residence, but not a home. Despite Miss Bords and her staff meeting basic needs, they never could have been a replacement for the nurturing that came from a family bond. Marjorie's heart always knew that, but in recent days she ached intensely over the loss.

Her mind wandered to God. In His great love, He'd created family for life on earth. *And He'd offered her family with Him eternally.* Her heart twitched realizing again how negligent she'd become with His offer.

In rebuttal, a stubborn emotion tugged at that twitch— Anger. Why had God thought she'd be better off an orphan than a family member?

"Marjorie, meet Mrs. Jennings." Gordon directed his hand toward the lady.

"Mrs. Jennings, this is Marjorie. She works here now."

Marjorie grinned and took the frail hand extended to her as Gordon snapped the protective drape around the lady's thin neck. "Nice to meet you."

"Call me Shoug—spelled S.H.O.U.G.

Gordon laughed. "The name suits her. Mrs. Shoug Jennings is affectionately called the 'Pie Lady.'"

"Pie Lady? How sweet." Marjorie winked.

"Yes, I am famous in these parts for my pies. Sold them to restaurants and bakeries."

Marjorie snapped her finger. "Did you bring them to the orphanage too?"

"Why, yes, I did. Those dear children deserved some home baked goods."

They sure did.

"Did you work there?"

"Yes, and I grew up there."

"Oh." Her cold, manicured fingers reached from behind the drape and squeezed Marjorie's own. Silence threatened so Marjorie rescued the moment. "Your banana cream was my favorite."

"I'll make you one sometime."

"Yummy."

Gordon swiveled the chair around to face the mirror. "Same sassy style, Shoug?"

An aged chuckle escaped from Mrs. Jennings. "What a mouthful. And, yes. I've got to look my best for baking today."

Gordon explained. "Shoug gets access to the Hillhurst kitchen and staff every Monday to help bake pies for Turkey and Dressing Tuesday."

"And, now I have the secret spice for my apple pie—thanks to Gordon."

"Delicious." Marjorie wanted to pet the dear woman's cheek, so enraptured was the lady over baking.

"Ginger makes the difference. But don't tell my secret."

"My lips are zipped."

The radio went to a commercial promoting instant pudding. Mrs. Jennings clicked her tongue. "Instant pudding. Egregious."

Marjorie laughed. Her mind catapulted to a senior high vocabulary book—the last time she'd thought of that word.

Valene entered the salon from the staff door, a hint of barbecue clinging to her.

"Hi, Shoug. What's the pie going to be this week?"

"Apple."

"My favorite." Her boss motioned for Marjorie to follow her.

Inside the office, Valene handed her an envelope. "Half your paycheck. I thought you might appreciate the advance."

The bills seemed to burn through the envelope and heat Marjorie's skin. Goodness. "Thank you. I'm thrilled."

Her thanks collided with Valene's "Oh, you're welcome," as though the appreciation were expected, and the boss had moved on.

"Our next customer is a man. I've decided to let you shampoo his hair. He has very little, so you'll mainly be washing his head. I thought you might want to do something besides clean. I'll stand on the other side of the bowl and watch."

Marjorie raised up on her toes. "I'd love to do that." She'd worked here one full day, and not had one lesson at beauty school, yet Valene had decided to trust her. Pride surged through her.

They moved to the washbowl and her boss sat in the chair and demonstrated the correct position for the customer's neck.

"Here, sit and see how it should feel."

Marjorie did. The bottom of her skull rested against the curve in the porcelain bowl. Her feet rested on the floor. Valene pulled her up. "Now, Mr. Winkle is very stooped and short, so we'll adjust the chair this way. He drools. Part of his lip is missing from cancer. He keeps a hankie, but sometimes forgets to use it. Have a washcloth in your pocket to use if you need it." *Ugh.* Valene pulled up a lever on the side of the chair. "Place the step stool here for his feet to rest on. But be careful. You'll have to help him get situated so he won't trip over the stool."

Valene's attention moved to the interior entrance and Marjorie's eyes followed to see the elderly man shuffling through the doorway.

It couldn't be. The client coming into the shop was the same man Marjorie had seen wandering the hallway during her covert tour. His hands clutched a book. She hadn't noticed the other day, but the man's mouth was deformed on one side.

Her stomach dropped. Sure enough, Stewart walked in behind the stooped figure, his presence towering over the little man.

Valene skittered toward them and slid her arm in the crook of Mr. Winkle's elbow.

"Marjorie, this is Hezekiah Winkle." Gordon and The Pie Lady joined her in speaking hello. A thought invaded—for all she knew this man or any elderly man in town could be her grandfather. All her life she'd searched for resemblance in faces of people the age she thought her parents would be. Never had she thought to search for grandparents. She noted Mr. Winkle again. Nothing similar between them.

"Is it story day?"

"After your shampoo and haircut, you can sit in the corner story chair." Valene patted the man's arm. "And Marjorie," a grin spread across the woman's face, "this is my brother, Stewart."

Stewart Dixon's eyes widened when he put his attention on her. His lips curved. "Marjorie, do you remember me?"

She wanted to dash to the parking lot. "Uhm, from the hallway the other day."

"Right, but I think we went to elementary school together."

"Sorry. I don't recall you from school." She watched his shoulders droop then his jaw tighten. His response baffled her. Something about him raised her defenses.

"That's cool, even though I remember you."

"You and Mr. Winkle caught me giving myself a tour." She pointed as she spoke, "Though, I didn't know you were Valene's brother then."

Valene interjected, "Well, what a coincidence that y'all ran into each other. Surprised neither of you mentioned it." She shrugged.

"I wasn't sure it was the same person when I looked at your family picture last night." Marjorie felt her cheeks flush.

"I don't throw your name around, Sis."

Marjorie hoped she only thought about rolling her eyes.

Stewart turned his attention to Valene. "I'll be back for Mr. Winkle in a half hour." He kissed his sister on the cheek and raised his eyebrows at Marjorie. She gagged internally.

Marjorie helped her boss ease Mr. Winkle into the shampoo chair, then she carefully placed a towel around the man's neck for comfort. Before she could drape him, Hezekiah handed her his book. "It's story time."

She followed Valene's earlier lead. "After your shampoo and haircut."

"Mr. Winkle, Marjorie will read a chapter of your book in just a few minutes."

I will?

"Hand it to her so it won't get wet, please."

Hezekiah's hand trembled as he held the book out to Marjorie. She glanced at the cover, and her heart tendered toward him. "*Windy Hop Tales* by Clara James. She's the local author from nearby Layton." Her eyes surely twinkled. "This is one of my favorite books at the orphanage. She came and read to the children twice a year."

"Is it story time?" He dabbed his chin with a worn hankie. Marjorie suppressed a gag, determined to handle this client professionally and with care.

Marjorie patted the man's arm. "After your shampoo and haircut." She walked the book to the customer chair and laid it down with a measure of reverence.

Using careful movements, she moistened the man's head then lathered a dot of shampoo. For the first time in her life, Marjorie's fingers moved over the head of an actual client. Her insides quivered. *I was made for this.* Mr. Winkle would have a permanent place in her memories.

• • •

With Mr. Winkle gone and a third appearance of Stewart behind her, Marjorie swept hair from the floor and straightened Valene's station for her next client.

"Hey, Marjorie, could you check Mrs. Jennings's hair to see if it is set?" Gordon's request pleased her. "Sure." She leaned the broom against the counter then moved to lift the dryer dome. Mrs. Jennings didn't look up from the magazine she'd snatched from the table. She'd been ripping out recipes for ten minutes and evaluating them aloud. Marjorie grinned. Apparently, the woman talked to herself—in a volume she could hear while under the dryer.

The woman's hair felt stiff around the bristly curlers. Marjorie felt beneath each one before deciding that the hair was set. "I believe she's ready." Gordon stood at her side in two strides and quickly ran his fingers over the curlers. He smiled. "Good work."

Valene emerged from the stock closet with a can of hair spray. She wiggled it as she addressed Marjorie. "Wanda's favorite."

"Wanda is coming in again?" So soon.

"She comes three times a week. Saturday is wash and set. Monday is touch-up. Thursday is manicure. I think she feels at home in here."

Shoug Jennings announced her opinion. "Those are her activity nights. She must look her best." She didn't miss a rip as she spoke.

"I see." Marjorie giggled. *That's exactly why you are here.*

The client strode into the room. Not one hair out of place. How amusing. Would Valene comb out all of Wanda's hair and roll it again?

"Hello, Wanda." Valene hugged the woman before she sat down. Wanda's pale face contrasted her impeccable appearance. Marjorie hurried to the broom she'd left propped against the station counter.

Wanda's eyes darted toward Marjorie. "Poor practice. Leaving a broom so a customer can see it. Much less trip over it."

"I'll remember that." She swallowed and grabbed the broom and dustpan. "Good to see you again."

"I hope you haven't been in the way."

Marjorie bit her tongue to squelch a groan.

"She's proving to be a skilled addition to the shop. She's one you'd peg as a shining star back in the day."

Bless you, Valene.

"Well, you're a good judge of talent, but I prefer to form my own conclusions. Time will tell."

Wanda shooed Marjorie away with her hand. And like an obedient child, Marjorie scurried off.

Good, it was lunch break anyway. As she grabbed the break room door, Valene's voice rose. "Wanda, are you sick?" Marjorie hurried to shut the door, but didn't before Wanda vomited on the floor.

. . .

Daniel shifted his position to rest his back and elbows on the bleacher behind him. The gym smelled of body odor. He glanced at the banner displayed over the basketball hoop. "All County 1956." The junior high's one claim to athletic fame was the girls' basketball team that year. That achievement glared at the awkward teams every year since as they attempted to toss a ball into the basket.

He looked at his watch. How long could a committee debate the shade of blue before a decision would be made? He could care less if sky blue or navy-blue balloons adorned the gym doorways on dance night. He'd much rather know the number of balloons he'd be hanging.

"Sky blue it is." The committee chairwoman clapped her hands, her preferred shade having been selected. "Daniel was our tie-breaker." *I was?* He'd flippantly lifted his hand after hearing "raise your hand for this shade."

The chairwoman sugar coated her gloating. "Good to have you on the team." He gave a polite smile, then caught Martina Cortes' grin. He rolled his eyes at her; grateful she knew he didn't want to be involved with the dance.

"One last item." Surely the leader was joking. They should be adjourned. Hunger gripped him, and this meeting had taken his supper time before he headed for Hillhurst to teach his paint class.

"We'll need a bathroom monitor rotation schedule. One for the girls and one for the boys."

"Meaning I'll be standing outside the boy's room all night?" His hand scanned the group indicating he was the only male.

"No. It means someone needs to put the non-committee eighth-grade teachers on a schedule."

"I'll do it." Hunger could make a man say and do insane things.

"Excellent." Well, good.

"Meeting adjourned?" Daniel stood and stretched. Committee members snickered.

"Well, I suppose it is. That is today's last item."

Daniel grabbed his satchel and excused himself. Dashing to the parking lot, he tossed the satchel into the back seat of his car. He lowered the convertible top, pulled from the parking lot, and let wind blow the meeting from his mind. Despite the committee meeting, wondering if he'd see Marjorie again, and teaching, he hadn't been able to dismiss Conrad's telephone call last night. The contact irked him.

He and Conrad had been unlikely friends. Daniel had a good-sized social group that included a roommate who graduated ahead of him. When Conrad filled the dorm vacancy, the two of them fell into a comfortable stride and friendship. When the wedding was being planned, Conrad's kinship didn't outrank the former room-mate's, but resembled it enough to stand in his absence since he was overseas.

Daniel pulled out of the school parking lot and turned on the classical radio station, letting the harmonic chords trigger his creative thoughts. After all, music is a painting without a canvas. Tonight, the students—he chuckled—the elderly students would be copying his image of the small creek and waterfall he'd discovered while kayaking in Austin.

A glance at the orphanage in his rearview mirror brought Marjorie front and center in his mind. He imagined her standing there, reverent, during the procession. Truth was, he figured he'd never see her again. Her working at The Wright Do came as a pleasant surprise.

He'd blown it in the Hillhurst parking lot Saturday.

Yep—he was a mere human who floundered and flubbed from time to time.

He switched radio stations to his favored rock and roll and the upbeat sounds gave him confidence. His fingers drummed the steering wheel while his stomach growled above the tunes.

. . .

Daniel slipped the last paintbrush back into his satchel. The scent of oil paints lingered in the air, caught in the corners of the boxy room with square tiles. He shook his head, recalling tonight's interpretations of his original piece. He didn't teach this class to see a good replica. Fulfillment came when creativity brought the residents to life. He'd missed Wanda Darden tonight. She'd never missed an art session. Somehow the atmosphere deflated without her curtness.

But Mrs. Darden was not the focus of his thoughts. Marjorie occupied his mind.

He gathered his supplies, turned off the Bach album, then scurried past the unfinished pieces left to dry. There was no time to load his supplies into his car before the beauty shop closed, so with full arms, he headed toward The Wright Do.

He grunted when he saw Gordon alone in the shop.

"Hi."

"Hi, Daniel. Here for a haircut?" The man glanced at his watch.

"No. I hoped to find Marjorie."

Gordon's eyebrows jumped up. "She just left. Probably still in the parking lot." He tilted his head toward the outer door.

"Thanks, man."

"I didn't know you knew her." Gordon's voice followed Daniel to the door.

"I don't," He looked back into the shop. "But I want to."

Only two cars remained in the lot, his and Gordon's. Daniel huffed. By what Gordon indicated, she couldn't have gone far. He scanned the road hoping he might see her behind a steering wheel. Instead, he noticed the figure at the bus stop and his breath hitched. He eased his belongings to the gravel.

"Marjorie?" Pebbles crunched beneath his heavy stride. The lady turned and smiled.

"Hi, Daniel."

She looked cute as all get out in those sunglasses. Daytime fading to evening shed a soft light on her complexion.

"What'cha doing?" Good grief—his shyest student might have asked a better question.

"I think I'm waiting on the bus." She tapped her finger on her chin.

He slid next to her on the bench.

"Car broken?"

"Don't own one."

Good! He would have to offer a ride to and from the diner if she accepted his invitation.

"I see."

They smiled at the same time. Perhaps he'd not lost all dignity at their previous encounter.

A car honked as it passed, but Daniel kept his focus.

"Join me for supper? I'm headed to Rosie's Diner."

"I'd love to."

She'd love to!

"My treat."

Her forehead wrinkled. "You don't have to..."

"I'd be honored to treat you."

"Your treat."

Daniel had driven the route to Rosie's Diner countless times, and he was a mature man who'd been moments from being married. Yet, the female sitting next to him in the convertible turned this trip into a first-time adventure and him into a man eager for a new direction.

A gentle rhythm buzzed around him, and he wouldn't swat it away. Curiosity. Not just physical. No denying that existed. But curiosity over the heart of the lovely creature. Her strengths. Her talents. Her struggles. Her beliefs. The things that fluttered inside her and took flight in laughter or tears. He sounded like a poet rather than an artist.

He shifted his eyes between her and the road. In this moment, Candace seemed nothing more than a passing shadow. Familiarity had led them like unsuspecting children to pronounce their mutual love. Now, the unfamiliarity of Marjorie intrigued him.

Words flowed between them.

He sang along to the rock and roll on the radio while her torso bopped to the beat. Wisps of hair blew into her face and over her sunglasses. She hung her arm out the window while her hand pushed against the wind.

When the "rock around the clock" song blared from the radio, she blended her deep voice with his.

The menu at Rosie's Diner suited many a pallet, ranging from spaghetti to corn dogs. Round tables with red chairs filled the center while booths with navy blue seats lined the walls. Though a juke box filled the corner, customers knew that Rosie preferred chatter fill the air. He opened the car door for Marjorie.

"What's your favorite thing on Rosie's menu?"

"I don't know. I've never eaten here."

He rubbed his chin. "Well, I reckon I like it all."

She grinned, and dropped her sunglasses into her purse. The waitress passed by several seats before placing them at the back of the diner.

His senses took in nothing but her. Ironic that a man could think himself in love enough ready to stand at an altar, then after being jilted realize he hadn't been. The truth that they weren't in love must have niggled at Candace whether she realized it or not, so she flew the coop. Maybe she was as much a victim of their awful wedding plans as he had been. Perhaps she'd done them both a favor by abandoning him.

He and Marjorie chatted through the menu as they made their selections. She loved grilled cheese. He preferred cheeseburgers.

74

They both preferred tater tots over fries. She'd pass on Swedish meatballs any day.

"I could feast on those every day."

"Yuck. Everyday?"

He patted his stomach. "I suppose Swedish meatballs are an acquired taste by us frozen dinner connoisseurs."

"I could eat my weight in mashed potatoes and banana splits," Marjorie teased.

The waitress interrupted the banter as she set down the colas they'd ordered. "What'll you have?"

"I'll have the cheeseburger basket, and the lady chose the grilled cheese basket. Both with tater tots."

The waitress scribbled on her pad. "Coming up."

. . .

"Daniel?" Marjorie tapped the table. "Do you want my pickle? I'm not much of a fan." Her voice drew him from his thoughts. He reached into her sandwich basket and pulled out the spear. "Yeah."

"So, the other person I helped today besides the Pie Lady and Mr. Winkle was Wanda. Bless her heart. She got sick right there in her chair. Valene cleaned it up."

"Oh, so that's why she missed my class."

"So, you know her?"

"Yep. Mrs. Darden is an art student."

"Darden?"

"Yeah."

"Wanda Darden?"

He laughed and pushed her cola glass toward her. "Take a sip. You look puzzled."

"Any relation to Troy Darden from the parade?"

"Mother and son."

"I had no idea."

"Why should you?"

"Well, good point."

"Even if you knew her name, you still may not have known that Wanda Darden was related to Troy Darden." He bit into his cheeseburger.

"Another good point. No wonder you're a teacher." That comment made him smile.

"I noticed there was only one car behind the hearse. So, Wanda has no family?"

"He was an only child."

"What about her husband?"

"I think he died when Troy was a little boy."

"No wonder she's so ornery."

Daniel laughed.

"She looked pitiful when they wheeled her back toward her room."

"Wheeled her?"

"Valene insisted."

"Yeah, they go way back. You know that story?"

"That story I do know." She held up a tot and popped it in her mouth. He could paint that happy face.

This non-date might be the best date he'd ever had.

Moments later, he ordered a banana split to share then watched as she sunk her spoon into the hot fudge—again and again.

The diner was near closing time. Speaking of it, he'd stop time if he could. Within moments, the night stars were witness to their continued camaraderie as he pulled onto the street.

"So, which way to your place?"

"Oh, Benton Street. I'm staying with Valene until I find a place I can afford."

He nudged her arm with his elbow. "Parents kick you out?"

"Yep. Nineteen years ago." Her hand touched his shoulder and he glanced her way. "I grew up at the orphanage."

Idiot. Buffoon. Ignoramus. Could he embarrass himself or this woman any more than he just had?

"I had no idea."

She offered a smile. "Why should you?"

The Deja vu amused him. "Well, good point. But, my joke stinks. Do you know what happened to your parents?'

"No."

Silence followed, and Daniel didn't want her to clam up. He pressed further.

"What do you know?'

"I was told my mother loved me. She left a sealed envelope with papers in it at the orphanage. I've never opened it."

"You chose not to?"

"Right. In fact, the thought of it scares me."

"Tough decision. Reckon an explanation in those papers might help you?"

"It might. But knowing might also make things harder for me."

This classy chassis next to him had a tough break. Sometimes life's allotments seemed unbalanced. Maybe he could help fix one of her problems.

"Back to your dilemma of an affordable place to live...I might have a solution."

"Don't tell me you're a teacher, a painter, and a real estate agent?"

"Nope. No selling for me. My family has a room to rent at their house." *My old bedroom.* "It's on the other side of town. I could set up a meeting for you."

The possibility of seeing this girl in his family home—sleeping in his old bed—well, he just shouldn't go there.

She tossed him one question after another, her lips spreading in a grin and her eyes sparkling.

Yep, he'd love to capture her animation on a canvas.

"I'll telephone my folks tonight. If it's okay with them, then I'll look up Valene's phone number and call you to confirm a meeting."

"I have her number in my purse. I can give it to you. One more thing. Does your family have cats?"

"Nope. My parents are allergic. And so am I."

"Me too." She squeezed his wrist for a second. He'd have preferred sixty of them.

"I should tell you that my dad is a lawyer. He may ask for a character reference."

"He should." She gasped. "I mean, he should get one on any potential renter."

"I understood what you meant. You sure you want to live with my family if it works out?"

"Yes. I think I get what you're saying. Not much privacy. But that'd be the case with any room I rented."

"They're good folks. You don't need to worry about that. We all go to church every week. If you don't have one, you can join us."

She smiled. *I need church.*

"I'd like that."

He smiled in return, unsure if her answer implied she had no church she attended on her own.

"I'm a Christian, Daniel. Honestly, I got out the habit of church. I'd already decided I needed to get back in."

"Well, we'd love to have you join us—whether you rent my parents' room or not."

"I think if they'll have me, I'll take that room. Daniel, the price is unbelievable. I checked on one of those furnished apartments. The leasing girl, Candace, seemed surprised I turned down leasing a unit."

The car jerked. Marjorie squeaked.

"Did you say Candace?"

"Yep. Don't know why I remember the name. Maybe because she looked close to my age. You know her?"

Would his past ever leave him alone? He wished Candace would just move away—again.

"Yeah."

Moisture beaded on his forehead.

"I almost married her."

7

Marjorie leaned forward in her seat and stretched her back. She rolled her head side to side to release tightness. Her aching tail bone throbbed against the metal chair. She glanced at her watch. Lunch break had been two hours ago.

The first morning of beauty school had been filled with orientation, uniform selection and care guidelines, then course assignments. Her first class began right after the noon meal.

She glanced at the textbook and spiral notebook on the small desk. A strong odor seeped in from the room next door. Students more advanced than she were learning about hair tinting and bleaching. She'd spent the morning learning professional basics and the importance of personal appearance.

"I'd like for everyone to stand and pick a partner." Marjorie welcomed the instructor's command and stood. She glanced at the student next to her. "Want to partner, Evelyn?" The petite redhead yawned, then accepted.

"You are going to examine your partner's posture and walk. Successful cosmetologists learn to stand and walk correctly. This will help you look young, thinner, and smarter."

Who knew the secret to success lay in posture and gait? Marjorie recalled Valene standing tall and erect behind her salon chair as she worked and also moving gracefully through her house. At the very least, maybe she'd learn how to keep her feet from aching after a long day at the salon. All the better if others viewed her as younger, thinner, and smarter.

While Evelyn stood still Marjorie held two yardsticks taped together next to her to see where she might be slumping or pooching. Knowing she'd be judged next; Marjorie tightened her midsection. Her crisp white uniform, a provision of the scholarship, felt no looser. Good. Maybe she didn't need to worry about a protruding middle.

That fact that Daniel had planned to marry another woman did worry her slightly. Marjorie couldn't deny the attraction between them, but now she wondered if she should ignore it. In her mind, couples adopted orphans when they couldn't have their first choice—a child of their own. Was it the same between men and women? If so, she didn't want to be his second pick. She could be his friend instead.

An image of Candace in the leasing office came to mind. What had she said? "Fall in love. Then pay the price." Once her name came up last night, Daniel had briefly explained that she'd cancelled their marriage the evening before the wedding. How ironic the words seemed, knowing Candace had deserted Daniel.

Evelyn's voice interrupted her fretting. "Where do you live?"

"Uhm, I'm in between places right now. The person I live with has cats, and I'm allergic. I'm looking for a place." The deal with Daniel's parents wouldn't be settled until she met them tonight to discuss arrangements. And if she felt awkward being around them, then she would need another place.

"Got family nearby?"

"No."

"Oh, where you from?"

"Here."

Marjorie watched as Evelyn opened her mouth then shut it. Of course, it didn't make sense to be from here and yet have no family around. She did not want to explain her orphan status. The truth would likely come out eventually. Until then, she'd rather go without the looks of pity.

Evelyn's eyes shifted toward the floor that looked dingy against their white shoes. Marjorie might as well spill the news.

"I grew up at the orphanage here in town."

And like the procession for Troy Darden she'd watched go by, emotions paraded over Evelyn's face. Shock. Intrigue. And pity. The orphan parade always ended with pity.

"I'm sorry."

"It's not your fault."

A nervous laugh preceded Evelyn's words. "I guess not. Seriously, if you need a place to crash with me and my cousin for a couple of nights, you can. No cats or tobacco."

"Thanks."

"Now, let's look at your posture."

If composure were measurable like posture, Marjorie's would be textbook perfect—head up, chin in, and shoulders down, though staying composed required worn and weary effort.

The exercise ended. Both of them poised and proper and one of them humiliated, they returned to their seats as the instructor pulled down a chart of the human skeleton.

. . .

Marjorie inhaled a deep breath, welcoming the scent of the crepe myrtle trees outside the beauty school. In her childhood imaginings, the perfect family home had crepe myrtles in the yard. She enjoyed the scent of shampoo, perm solution, and hairspray that filled the interior of the building, but the change relaxed her. Shifting her textbook, notebook, and a bag, she reached into her purse for her sunglasses. Then she spotted Daniel sitting in his flip-top tapping a beat on his steering wheel. His eyes were fixed in her direction. He raised a hand and waved, then opened the door and scurried to the passenger side.

"Afternoon. Mighty fine uniform."

"Thank you. One thing's for sure, I don't have to buy shoes for the salon now. These stylish utility shoes are comfortable."

He closed her door. "Sit back and relax." He slipped inside the driver seat. "Got an appetite?"

"You don't have to feed me again."

"I'm not. My family is."

"I thought I was meeting them about renting the room."

"You are. Over supper. "

"You didn't mention a meal."

"Sorry about that."

She blew out a breath. The clothes she'd worn to school were crumpled in the bag. If she'd known she was gonna sit at a supper table with his family, she'd at least have folded them neatly and changed back into them.

"I wish you'd told me."

"What's the big deal?" With that comment she noticed him squeeze his forehead. Maybe their Candace conversation last night bothered him too.

"I don't know. I could have prepared."

"Prepared?"

"Yeah."

He shook his head back and forth. In turn, she pursed her lips and stared ahead. Other than the wind whipping in her ear, seconds of silence squeezed between them until he cleared his throat.

"Are you hungry?"

"Yes."

"Then you're prepared."

She laughed, and with it, her irritation slipped away. But she wished it hadn't. Because that irritation made it easier to ignore the attraction. But since she was too weary to pout, had a great day, and sat next to a dreamboat, she asked about his day instead and learned he'd had a tough one. She flung her arm into the wind and let it whip through her fingers.

"On top of the disrespectful student and the one who failed a test for the first time, my day ended with a dance committee meeting." He rolled his eyes.

"What a blast!"

"Not at all."

"You party pooper. Daniel, what do you do to relax?"

He whisked the air. "I paint."

She elbowed him. "You should start painting a landscape tonight."

He smiled. "I've been planning a portrait of a beauty school student."

Her heart somersaulted.

They fell into another silence and though she'd rather fill it, she let it sit. Maybe he needed the quiet.

When Daniel turned onto a gravel driveway, Marjorie felt her jaw drop. Picture perfect described Daniel's childhood home. Even the crepe myrtle trees that she loved stood in the yard. He opened the door for her and she stood next to it. "Welcome to my parents' pad."

She covered her mouth with both hands and stood on tiptoes. She wanted to live here.

Surely, she could live here and just be friends with the handsome history teacher.

"She's here!" A high-pitched voice announced the gangly pre-teen girl running their way.

Daniel guided Marjorie forward. "Tali, meet Marjorie. Marjorie, this is my younger sister."

Marjorie made eye contact. "It's nice to meet you."

"I like your uniform."

"Well, thank you."

"Maybe sometime, if you decide to live here, you could practice on my hair."

"That would be fun."

From inside the house, a man, woman, and young boy made their way to the front porch that hosted two navy aluminum rockers and a small table. A brown mat welcomed folks at the door. Daniel introduced the rest of his family. "These are my parents, Leland

and Lucy. This squirt is my brother Theo." As he pronounced each name, Marjorie sensed a layer of homelessness fall to the ground.

An hour or so later Daniel and his siblings cleared the table and headed to the kitchen for clean-up. Marjorie's insides fluttered at the sight of him doing woman's work and the sound of him laughing with Tali and Theo. She stood and followed his parents on the tour of the home. Every room she saw boasted at least one of Daniel's paintings.

A family photograph in the hallway caught her eye. A young Daniel held the hand of a woman who resembled him, but wasn't Mrs. Buckler. Perhaps it was an aunt. He was a cute kid.

"This would be your room." Mrs. Buckler opened the door and Marjorie stepped into a teenage boy's world. Daniel—as was—permeated the room. Paintings from a younger hand, high school and college pennants, and a display of army men dared her to feel at home here. "Now, since I wasn't sure if we would rent to a male or female, I've left the room untouched." Mrs. Buckler rested her hand on Marjorie's arm. "Our first order of business will be paint, then new decor, and a bedspread." Daniel's father released a mock groan. "Now, Leland, you know we talked about this." The man smiled.

Marjorie's heart fluttered. "Well, I'd even appreciate the room as is."

"Tsk. That won't do. I've needed Daniel to clear his stuff for a while." She chuckled. "What's your favorite color?"

"Blue."

"Perfect—that's mine too. This will be fun."

"Mr. & Mrs. Buckler, do you need me to give you a character reference?"

The wife looked at the husband. Mr. Buckler cleared his throat. "I'm a lawyer and had my law office check with the orphanage and the police department today. One can't be too careful when opening up their home."

"I agree." She did, though she hadn't anticipated a behind-the-scenes investigation.

She surveyed the bedroom one more time. A room of her own in a favorite color. Her thoughts wondered back to the conversation with Mr. Hurst. Yes, the Good Lord had provided.

· · ·

By the time Marjorie and Daniel left his parents' home, evening had turned to bedtime. The radio released muffled rhythms as though it were drifting to sleep. The man who'd opened his family to her still needed to point out the bus stops. The stops she'd use once she rose, warm and rested from his childhood bed, gobbled his mother's breakfast, and let out a see-you-tonight as though what was his now belonged to her.

He lifted his hand from the steering wheel. What would she think if he held hers? *Confusion is a wearisome companion.*

Instead, his hand stifled a yawn. She smiled. The man had talked about the classwork he had to grade tonight. When did he ever find time to relax and paint?

"Your family is really nice."

"Thanks. Lucy is my step-mother. My mom died when I was six years old."

"I'm sorry." *No matter the reason, the loss of a mother is sad.*

"I noticed a picture in the hallway of you and a woman. Was that your mom?"

"Yes. It was taken not long before she died. Tali and Theo are half siblings. But only on paper, not right here." He tapped his heart.

"They're adorable."

"You met them on a good day."

"That's not nice."

"You're right. I was teasing. They are both great kids."

Feeling comfortable with Daniel's family both soothed and surprised her. Of course, she realized that once she moved in Sunday and started living in their space, awkwardness could set in. Not that she wasn't used to sharing space. But institutional space and a family home wouldn't likely compare.

"Looks like you're replacing me, Marjorie."

"Huh?"

"In the family."

She swatted at him. He yelped.

"Don't you know you're irreplaceable to them?"

He grinned.

"We barely know one another, but..." She pointed back and forth in the space between them.

He mimicked her motion. "I'd like to change that."

A smile pinched her cheeks red as it spread from ear to ear. "What I was going to say before you interrupted me, is that we barely know one another, but I'm glad we're friends."

"Hum, I've already got plenty of friends, Marjorie."

He slowed and pointed. "This is the stop for the beauty school. Bus comes every half hour. Any questions for me, friend?"

So many.

"None."

"Good. On to the next stop."

The convertible moved forward then made a left turn. Daniel passed the next bus stop she saw and continued driving. She listened as he sang along with the radio. The man couldn't carry a tune.

Though she'd never had to pay attention to miles because she'd never driven, Marjorie soon suspected they'd traveled far beyond walking distance of the Buckler home.

"Daniel?"

"Yeah?"

"I think we passed the next bus stop, way back yonder."

"I know."

"You did that on purpose?"

"Yes. I had another purpose in mind." He turned and looked at her.

Marjorie gasped, uncertain if the source was shock or anticipation with a hint of shame. He wanted to take advantage of her.

Daniel's face paled, then reddened. "No. Not that, Marjorie. My purpose was to have more time with you."

She sighed, uncertain if the source was relief or disappointment with a hint of shame.

Daniel jerked the car into a U-turn. "I hope I didn't scare you. I can be a dad blame idiot sometimes."

Marjorie laughed. "I like spending time with you too, Daniel." She reached and turned up the radio. "But you've got papers to grade, and I gotta get back in time to tell Valene I'm going to skedaddle."

Other than Daniel pointing out the bus stop for her work, the convertible carried the pair to Valene's residence in comfortable silence.

. . .

A car Marjorie didn't recognize sat in Valene's gravel drive. Daniel parked behind it, and before Marjorie could protest, he'd hoofed his way to her car door and opened it. The hint of sadness at saying goodbye took her aback, despite the embarrassing misunderstanding about his motives. She grabbed the bag with her change of clothes in one hand and let him pull her up with the other. Seconds of silence hovered in the air. Perhaps he didn't want to say goodbye either. Well, of course he didn't. That was the whole reason for the embarrassing situation. He closed the door.

She blew out a breath. "Thanks for everything you did today and arranged for me."

"Glad it worked out. Good luck with Valene."

"Oh, I think she'll be relieved. I'm pretty sure she is just being extra nice to me. She only had a few days in mind."

"I can walk you to the door." He motioned toward it.

"I'm fine. And, you, Mr. Buckler, have papers to grade." He smiled and made his way back to the driver side.

They said their goodbyes and she walked to the front door, touched that he didn't pull away until she walked inside.

How nice to feel protected.

A white feline rubbed against her leg when she entered. Marjorie shifted her leg away from the cat as she took in the scene. No secret admirer or best friend visited her boss—just Stewart. Sitting on the couch with the other cat perched in his lap, he looked over his shoulder

Valene was nowhere in sight. A wave of nausea moved over her.

"Well, we meet again. Welcome home." Stewart drew out the last word. The sound of fingernails on a chalkboard aggravated less. Shame on her, but she flat out did not like this man. Ugh, and to think she'd slept in his room.

"Are you staying here tonight?"

"Are you?" He retorted.

"Yes."

"Then, no, I'm not." He rolled his eyes.

Valene emerged from the hallway in a robe and met her with a wide smile. "How'd it go?"

Marjorie felt relief at Valene's greeting. The woman was a good person.

"Yeah, how'd it go?" Stewart rose as he spoke. Her brother on the other hand irritated her.

Valene hooked her arm through Marjorie's. "I want to hear about it." The gesture felt friendly, almost sisterly, at least she imagined it so. They sat at the small kitchen table.

"Well, it went real good. I'm going to move in this coming Sunday afternoon if that's okay with you." Valene lifted the lid of a plastic storage container and pulled out a brownie. "Sure, that works." She handed the brownie to Marjorie. "Tell me about the house."

Marjorie explained the arrangements, and when she mentioned the room would be redecorated just for her, Valene put a hand over her heart. "Marjorie, how exciting. What color did you pick?"

"Blue."

Stewart moved away from the counter where he'd been standing and pulled out a chair at the table. "Need help moving?"

"No. My belongings fit in a suitcase, and maybe an extra box. But thanks."

He looked at her, then cleared his throat. "You really don't remember me from school, do you?" She didn't and she'd rather keep things that way. Within her line of vision Valene's cat clock moved its eyes back and forth, keeping time with its tail.

"Oh, Stewart, remember. You went by your nickname in elementary school." Valene's reminder hinted at prodding. "Tell her what you were called."

"Si."

Marjorie cringed internally. Ugh. She remembered Si.

The boy with one name.

"Stewart Irving Wright," Valene interjected.

Si. The boy who threw-up in first grade homeroom every day for a month. "A nervous stomach," the teacher had explained. In her first-grade reasoning, the explanation did nothing to alleviate the stench in the classroom or the splatters on her shoes because she was seated to his left where he bent and deposited his breakfast on the tile floor. Memories of the custodian wiping the mess with a mop and running it through the ringer on a bucket made her queasy.

Si, the odd boy who in second-grade left presents on top of her desk. A set of jacks. A deck of Old Maid cards. A ponytail ribbon. A drug store brand of cologne at Christmas. A small heart of candy on Valentine's Day. Each gift had embarrassed her and earned her taunts from the pretty girls in the classroom. Even then, Marjorie realized Si was the least liked boy in their grade. His reputation, her heritage, and his quirkiness created the ideal formula for teasing.

Thank goodness no fellow students knew about the kiss.

Humiliation leapt from its resting place and began pounding in her brain. Oh goodness, how much does Valene know?

"So, do you remember him now?" Valene grinned, and Marjorie thought the glimmer in her eyes must be the hope she held that some soul was attracted to her relative. The employee looked her boss in the eye—this woman had done much for her in such a short time. The past was the past, and she didn't want to sacrifice the present for it. Valene didn't seem to know about Stewart's childhood behavior toward her.

"I sure do." She forced a smile.

The man cleared his throat. "But I bet you didn't forget about the boy who was sick for a month." He winked, and the gesture made her stomach turn.

Hopefully that's all Si would make public around the kitchen table.

"As much as I tried, —nope, I couldn't forget." She tapped her forehead, then took a breath.

"Why was your stomach so nervous back then?"

He glanced at Valene. "I had a digestive condition."

"Oh. I'm sorry about that. Is it better now?" She tore a small piece from her brownie and rolled it between her fingers.

"Yes. It's been better for many years."

Valene rose from her chair. "Well, it's late. Stewart, show yourself out, and make sure to turn off the television." She gathered her two cats in her hands. "Marjorie, I'll see you in the morning. Congratulations on your new place." Her boss headed toward the hall.

Marjorie rose to toss the rest of her brownie into the trash, but Stewart took it from her. He tossed the brownie then proceeded to wash the plate. She wished he would just leave.

"Well, good night, Stewart."

He turned from the sink to face her. "Wait." He placed the plate on the counter and tossed the dish towel over his shoulder. "I'd like for us to go out. Get to know each other again. No jacks, no cards, this time."

The man had no idea how unpleasant his manner was to her.

"Why would I want to go out with the person who yanked me behind the gym and forced a kiss on me?"

He blew out breath. "You remember."

"I can't forget something so humiliating."

"I was a third-grade punk." He leaned in. "My apology. I know how to treat a woman now. And I think you're hot."

You're not.

"Marjorie, we're not in elementary school anymore. Go on a date with me. I'd like that."

"I wouldn't."

Marjorie shoved her chair under the table and did an about-face. She had to force herself not to run to her bedroom.

Wait—his bedroom.

Of all the things he'd offered her and she'd turned down, how'd she end up sleeping in the house where he lived?

8

Marjorie nudged the jar of cotton balls a half-inch on the manicure table, then surveyed her work. Towel, instruments, jar of sterilizer, finger bowl. She lifted her classroom textbook from the patron chair and checked the example photo. Perfect.

She released a sigh. Mrs. Darden was due in for a wash and set. If she knew Marjorie had disinfected and prepped the manicure table, she'd likely bring a ruler and measure the placement of each item.

Mrs. Darden and one more client were the last appointments for the busy Saturday. She hadn't seen Mrs. Darden since Monday when the lady had been ill. At supper Thursday night Valene had said the older woman still looked pale when she came in that day for her manicure.

Marjorie rubbed the back of her neck, then straightened the magazines in the small basket between the hair dryers. She tossed the one Mrs. Jennings had ripped to pieces. As much as she'd love to sit and thumb through the pages of a latest edition, she didn't want Mrs. Darden to walk in and assume she slacked off. Of course, Valene wouldn't mind, and that's whose opinion mattered. She grabbed a magazine, and just in case Wanda walked in, she headed into the break room with it. The whirr of the washing machine reminded her she had one more load of towels to dry and fold once she'd observed Valene do the manicure.

Her boss expressed nothing but confidence and appreciation to Marjorie. She smiled, recalling the scene from earlier this afternoon when she'd bounded into the shop, tired from class, but exhilarated.

"We're learning about manicures and nails. I love it!"

"I think you're quite talented already with nails." Valene had paused her scissors mid-air to make the statement.

"Well, I could never argue with my boss."

When Valene had suggested "the beauty school student" set up the manicure station, said student had bounced on her toes. Work life proved to be better than she'd imagined, but living with Valene had felt a bit too close for comfort. Thankfully, she hadn't seen Stewart since Tuesday.

She hadn't seen Daniel Buckler either. She missed her friend-not-boyfriend. Hopefully he'd missed her too. Her skin tingled at the thought of him.

Truth was, she'd had no time for anything but school and homework and couldn't have afforded time with him anyway.

She'd certainly cross paths with the artist tomorrow after church time because he would be driving her for the move into his family home. But with perfect timing, she could see him tonight after he taught his art class.

Marjorie flipped to an article on fall decorating ideas just as Gordon's voice seeped under the laundry room door. "Afternoon, Stewart."

Ugh.

"Hi, Gordon. Is Valene here?"

"She's getting something from her car."

Marjorie tuned in to the conversation when she heard Wanda's name. She was sick again and wouldn't make her appointment.

"See you later." Stewart's voice announced his departure.

Marjorie closed the magazine and walked into the shop. She'd go ahead and shut down Valene's station for the day. Gordon looked up from his last client and suggested Marjorie see if the manicure patron could come early. If so, they could close up shop an hour early tonight.

She strode into the office, thumbed through the Rolodex, then dialed the client's room. Marjorie chuckled as she exited the office and shut the door.

"She coming?" Gordon was now alone in the shop.

"As soon as her soap ends in five minutes and she gets her teeth put in. And as long as we don't mind her coming with no makeup on."

Gordon laughed.

Soon her boss soaked the tips of curled fingers suffering with arthritis. What a lesson Valene had set up for Marjorie. She watched the professional handle each finger with tenderness and slow movements. A textbook may give written pointers, but Marjorie knew experience was teaching her far more.

Her mind slipped to Daniel. Could he paint these hands and somehow bring out the life they had lived? As the manicure neared the end, Valene covered the nails with a light peach shade that brought dignity to the aged hands. Marjorie caught the client's eye and smiled. "Beautiful." And though she referred to the nails, she'd captured the moment as well.

. . .

As Marjorie strode the hall toward the art class, her heart stirred. Maybe the tenderness of the manicure session still lingered. Her first impression of Hillhurst—blaring televisions, dull colored walls, and residents that seemed but a shadow of those thriving outside these walls—had changed. She was stirred by the reality that Hillhurst was the last earthly home for souls nearing life's end, and tenderness for them resonated through the hallways. Other than Miss Bords' confession of favoritism toward her, Marjorie had never sensed such care at the orphanage. The thought saddened her. A little tenderness might have softened the harshness of institutional life. The orphanage could have held glimmers of hope and a future as Hillhurst held glimmers of the past and goodbyes.

She located the classroom and peeked in the small window on the closed door. Ten or so students with their backs to her brushed color onto a canvas. She leaned in for a closer look, and her mind stilled. Daniel had his students painting a sunset. His original, perched front and center, displayed gorgeous shades of amber, pinks, and violet over a small lake.

"Marjorie."

She huffed. In her moments of reflection, she'd not given a thought to encountering Stewart in the hallways.

"Hi." Her eyes never left the classroom.

"Guess you got done early, with Wanda sick."

"We sure did. I think Valene is visiting her now."

"And you are..."

She rolled her eyes, then turned toward him. "Looking in on the art class."

"My bet is you're looking at the art teacher."

"Haven't seen him." Indeed, she hadn't. He was out of view before she'd looked away.

Stewart moved toward her, and his shoe squeaked against the floor. "I'm driving back to Waxee in a jiffy. When I'm back in town next week, maybe you'll reconsider us. We can meet up after work and see a movie."

"Stewart, no thanks. Please don't make this awkward for both of us."

His lips tightened to a straight line. "I want a shot at making you smile." He did an about face. "Goodbye. And congratulations on your new place."

"Thanks." How happy she'd be to no longer borrow his room.

She refused to look his way, and when his footsteps faded, she entered the room, closed the door, and took an empty seat at the back of the room.

Daniel didn't seem to notice her entry. He faced the opposite direction and leaned toward a hefty man with a white, burr cut. "Use the side of the brush for a sharper line." She noticed the aged student turned his brush. "Yes, like that. Now, apply less pressure than you did for the broad strokes." Daniel watched the student for a moment, then patted his shoulder. "That's a good tree branch."

Daniel Buckler seemed in his element as a teacher and an artist.

The object of her attention turned, and Marjorie waved. The man waved back and grinned. Marjorie snickered. His face resembled the photo of ten-year-old Daniel she'd seen hanging in his parents' home. Good thing she sat in a chair, because the effect of that boyish look made her light-headed. He introduced her as the new employee at The Wright Do. She nodded. "It's real nice to meet y'all."

For the rest of the session, Marjorie sat enamored by the setting. A quiet hum of conversation and gentle laughter came from some of the students, while others seemed lost in their own creative world. Classical music drifted quietly from a record player. Meanwhile, Daniel moved from student to student, giving instruction and encouragement until it was time to clean up.

A bustle of activity erupted as students cleaned brushes, admired one another's work, and placed their canvases to one side of the room before they scurried out in an array of groupings. Some nodded, some spoke a goodbye. Two women stopped in front of her. Marjorie stood. Each woman took hold of one of her hands. "Seems to be a fine young man," the taller of the two drawled. The quiet one patted her hand, and before Marjorie could respond, slipped through the doorway."

"I see you met The Sisters." A scent of chalk, paint, and early morning cologne accompanied Daniel as he stood before her.

"They made sure I knew you are a fine person." Marjorie slipped a strand of hair behind her ear.

"I won't argue with wisdom. Let me grab my things."

"I'll help."

He squeezed her hand. "I'm glad you stopped in."

"Me too." Her hand tingled from the brief contact.

Marjorie followed him around, taking whatever gadget he handed her. She paused at his artwork the students had been replicating.

"Daniel, this scene is lovely. The colors are gorgeous." She touched the violet hue behind the painted sun. "You are so talented."

"Thanks. That's the pond behind my neighborhood. I caught the sunset just right one evening, and the vividness stuck in my head. I had to paint it."

"That blows my mind."

He directed her toward the door.

"Do you ever participate in art shows?"

"Sometimes."

"Do you sell a lot?"

"I sell enough to feel good about it."

She nodded. "I'm glad."

They meandered their way through the halls. A hush settled in Hillhurst tonight. Residential doors were closed, the muffled television voices seeping under the closed doors. A few stragglers nibbling on sweets while the staff wiped tables graced the dining hall. The air felt warm.

"It's hot in here."

"The residents get cold, I figure."

Daniel opened the door to the parking lot, then they headed to his car. A crisp breeze brushed her shoulder and sent a chill up her arms. Crickets chirped and a horn beeped. A sliver of moon shone ahead of schedule.

"Could you slip this bag in the back seat?" He handed it over to her.

"Sure."

Marjorie heard the trunk close. If she didn't get to the bus stop within a minute or two, she'd likely miss it. She shuffled her feet in the gravel.

"Want to grab something to eat?"

She released a breath at his question. Had she been holding it?

"I'd love to. But quick—I have a lot of studying to do." She twisted her spandex watch band and it pulled a hair. *Ouch.*

"Quick it is. I've got tests to grade." He winked. "Hop in."

Gladly.

. . .

By the time they reached the burger joint, Daniel and Marjorie decided they should study and work at the library. It took little convincing for either of them. He drove with one hand and ate his burger with the other as they headed toward the library near the local high school. Marjorie balanced her grilled cheese, their shared tater tots, and both colas while they listened to the evening news on the radio. As they neared the school, Marjorie saw the stadium lights were on and rolled down the window.

"Go Broncos!"

Daniel laughed and turned down the radio. "Cool. You a football fan?" He took another bite.

Marjorie chuckled. "Yes, I'm a football fan."

She sang the university fight song at the top of her lungs, and Daniel joined in. Marjorie threw back her head and laughed.

"You are one fun chick, Marjorie Mullins." He wrinkled his burger paper in his fist and tossed it into the bag near her feet.

"Miss Bords is a UT alumnus. She listened to every game on the radio in the recreation room. Lots of us joined her because she served popcorn and colas. After the first quarter, most of the kids got ants in their pants and left, their bellies full. Me and a few others always stayed."

"Well, you know that's my alma mater too."

"I know."

"You do?"

"And you ran track in high school." She elbowed him. "I noticed the pennants and ribbons in your room. Uhm...my room."

"Not until tomorrow."

"If your mother had her way, it's already transformed to mine." She pointed at him before stuffing her trash into the drive-thru bag.

Daniel slurped his last drops of cola. "I'm homeless."

"Nope, just room-less, and you own a home, you goof."

Her stomach sunk when she saw his face pale. "Marjorie, I'm a dunce to make homeless jokes."

His chagrin charmed her. "That's kind, but don't worry. I've never been homeless. I've just never had a home."

Daniel kept silent, and Marjorie felt awkward, so she nudged his arm with her fist.

"You a fan of the newest Dallas football team? It's crazy we have two teams."

"A divided Big D. I may or may not switch my loyalty. It's too soon to decide."

"You're gonna hold out for the better of the two teams?" She tsked.

"You know me so well already." He drummed his fingers on the steering wheel, then pulled into the library parking lot. The stay was short-lived when they discovered the library closed for the night.

"Bummer. I forgot it closes early on Saturday."

Marjorie thought she'd crumble with disappointment. Had she gone directly to Valene's she could have withstood being alone tonight, but the loss of spending time with Daniel made that option unbearable. She knew her hostess went to the movie with friends tonight, so she couldn't invite him in.

Who was she kidding? She couldn't invite him into someone else's home anyway.

Sadness took her by surprise, pulsing through her as though she'd chugged it like a cola. Why couldn't her parents make a home with her, especially if her mother loved her, as Miss Bords indicated? The sealed envelope flashed in her mind's eye. If she read it contents, her mind would know. And so would her heart. That's what scared her. She'd coddled her disappointment into believing her parents hadn't left her by choice. The news in the sealed envelope could prove otherwise and reading it would remove the cocoon she'd built.

"We could head to my parents' house."

"Oh. That might pressure your mother" *And make me appear desperate.* "She might be doing last minute preparations."

"Right." Daniel shifted his feet. "Well, how about my place?"

"Uhm..."

"I'll open my garage door, turn on the light, and we can sit in lawn chairs. I've got a bug zapper thing."

He'd interrupted her "Uhm, yes."

What did her impulsive, unspoken, "yes" say about her?

Nothing.

Her response had everything to do with how she viewed Daniel.

"Good idea."

Good man.

Good looking.

Good grief—she was crazy over this guy.

Good luck being his friend.

• • •

"This?"

Daniel startled, and his foot slipped off the clutch, popping the convertible forward. His hand tightened on the gear stick that he hadn't yet moved to park.

He jerked his foot back onto the clutch and slid the convertible into park.

"What do you mean, 'this?'" His brows wrinkled.

She leaned forward and gestured toward his home.

"This house is yours?"

He turned off the ignition, faced her and offered her a smile, reluctancy in the gesture. Was it run down or unkempt for her feminine taste?

"Yes, this is home." He hid his uneasiness with the matter-of-fact tone.

"It's adorable."

He breathed out, and with no reluctance, smiled. He didn't know if "adorable" was an accurate description of his house, but it was on target for his companion.

"Thanks. Hey, let me get the garage door right quick." He eased himself out of the car. Marjorie's door opened and closed in unison.

"I've got to peek inside that front window. I'm dying to see inside."

His memory took a quick sweep of the rooms visible through that view. He wasn't messy, but he did tend to leave folded laundry on the couch for a day or two.

Recall told him the coast was clear.

"Help yourself." Daniel heard the gratification over her enthusiasm in his voice. He moved to the garage door and fingered his keyring for the key.

He scurried to the light chain and yanked on it, then moved to the back corner where blue mesh lawn chairs hung on a nail. Good thing he had two.

"Daniel, I have a better idea than this." Marjorie stood just inside the door, one hand holding her school work, the other on her hip. Light sparkled in her eyes—far more captivating than what the bulb put out. His fingers twitched. What a delight it would be to capture those blues on canvas.

He opened one of the chairs while the other rested against his leg. "What's that?"

"We can sit at your table inside by that front window."

A large grin supported her suggestion.

The woman had no idea what she did to his sanity. Her presence would fill every inch of the place. He'd likely never walk inside again without sensing her aura.

Like a jealous child, the memory of Candace being here days before jeered at him. *You're weak.*

He overturned the taunt, determined it would guard his resolve.

Though Marjorie was beautiful, he didn't think her suggestion aimed to trap him with enticement, unlike Candace.

"If you're cool with it, then so am I." He slapped the lawn chair shut and carried both back to the nail. Marjorie tugged the light off and they made their way back to the driveway. Just as he pulled down the garage door, the bug zapper emitted a shrill electric noise. Daniel caught Marjorie's eye. They laughed, and he grabbed his satchel from the back seat.

Mentally scanning his cabinets for something to offer her, Daniel settled on a can of shoestring potato chips. If their being here kept happening, and he would do everything he could to make sure it would, he'd need to keep his cabinets better stocked.

Marjorie arranged her things at the table, unknowingly taking his seat. He liked that. Most days he only ate breakfast at this table, sipping coffee while he ate. He'd do last minute grading or scan the newspaper. Supper and lunch belonged on a television tray.

"I can make coffee."

"You can?" She laughed.

"In an instant." He pointed to the jar of freeze-dried coffee on his counter.

"Just giving you a hard time. But, really, no thanks. I'm full."

He sat the can of chips between them, not missing her slightly raised lip at the gesture. He tried to settle into the quietness as they worked, but allowed himself a glance at her now and then.

"Want me to turn on the radio?"

"No thanks. I work better with quiet." She laid her book upside down and let out an exaggerated sigh. "I can't concentrate."

Join the club.

"I'm about to explode with curiosity. Can I see the rest of your house?"

He leaned back on two legs of the chair, a red pen in one hand. "Snoop all you want, but there's only a bathroom and two bedrooms down the hall. One is used as my art studio. None of them fluffy and pretty."

She jumped up with a start, and Daniel watched her bounce to the first door on the right. He chuckled, stuck a pencil between his teeth and tackled the next test.

A minute turned into five as Marjorie moved throughout his house, apparently pausing at each of his paintings on the wall. When she returned, satisfaction filled him as she gushed over his home and his art. When she settled back into her studies, he forced his heart to settle too.

She grabbed his hand and held it up so the palm faced him. She glanced at his hand, then back at her book.

"According to the textbook, you have square nails."

"I've often wondered." He spoke through the teeth that gripped his pencil.

The beauty school student looked up as she laughed then released his hand.

With his other hand, he snatched the pencil from between his teeth.

"Why do you chew on pencils, Square Nails?"

"Well, Funeral Lady, it helps me concentrate." He noted her eyebrows lift at the nickname.

"At least you're not biting those squares of yours."

He had no humorous retort, so enamored was he by their lightheartedness.

She patted his hand, which waited where she released it, apparently lingering for another chance at connection.

He laid his red pen on top of a test. "I like you, Marjorie Mullins."

"I like you, too." She closed her textbook. "Seriously Daniel, so much has happened emotionally over the last week, that I can't think straight."

"Is that good or bad?"

"Maybe a bit of both. The scholarship. A job. Starting school. A new place to live. All good, just so fast. And you—meeting you is definitely good. I've only known you a few days, but we seem so connected. I think I'm behaving like some junior high girl with goo-goo eyes for Mr. Buckler."

"No way. You're a fascinating woman. This connection is good. In fact, I think it's great.'

"But I can't move so fast."

"Neither of us should. We'll figure things out in time."

She smiled.

"And what's the bad stuff on your mind?"

"Two things. First, that stinking envelope that I've never opened."

"I'm sorry you're in this situation. But maybe the curiosity is actually harder than whatever the truth is."

"I'm scared."

"Man, I would be too. But don't let fear control you."

Thin lines formed on her forehead for a brief moment, then her face relaxed.

"I'll think about opening it."

'I'll pray about it for you."

She turned her head away from him slightly. Had he said something idiotic again?

"I'd appreciate those prayers. I kind of starved my faith. And well, now, I'm feeling the hunger pains."

"I'll pray about that too. You just need to start taking spiritual bites." He rolled his eyes at the corny analogy.

They both jerked when his telephone rang. Nuts! The call better be worth the interruption.

He slid from his chair and answered the phone.

"Do not call me." He hung up the receiver.

Marjorie sat with her lips pursed and eyes wide. For a second, he had forgotten he was not alone.

"Excuse my attitude." He moved to stand next to her chair. Those gorgeous blues looked up at him.

"Who called?" The inquiry surprised him, but he didn't shy from it.

"Candace."

"Oh."

His stomach churned when Marjorie tucked her head into her chest. He dropped to her eye level.

"I didn't expect the call. I don't want the call. I don't want Candace."

"That brings up my second bad thing. You were almost married."

"But I'm single."

"Not by choice."

"No, not then. But now. I don't love her."

Tears rolled down Marjorie's cheeks. "I don't want to be a replacement for anyone. No one's second choice."

"If you think I'd think that, you're mistaken. You are the choice I didn't know I had."

"But, you loved another woman. If she hadn't left, you'd be married to her."

"Yes, I would. And what a horrible mistake I'd be stuck with. Marjorie, when I said I didn't love Candace, I meant it. Thank goodness, she's not my wife."

"Daniel, are you crazy? There had to be something between you." Anger slipped into her tone.

"Yes. Familiarity. She was an assumption. The expected."

He might as well lay it all out there.

"Candace showed up here the other night. I could have had her back if I wanted to. I could have slept with her, but I'm waiting on my wife for that. The offer could not go unnoticed. I told her then that love is a choice and that I no longer choose to love her. Since then, I've realized I never loved her to begin with. I was just comfortable with her."

"I should have kept my feelings to myself. I'm such an idiot."

"Don't say that. Your feelings are doing some crazy good things to me right now."

"I bet you thought that about Candace too."

"What do you want me to say, Marjorie?"

"The truth."

"Yes, Candace and I had a long history. Yes, at one time I was attracted to her. But she didn't seep into my very being."

"Are you still attracted to her?"

"So, that's what you focused on." He rose and paced the kitchen.

"Are you?"

"I'm more than a biology specimen, if that's what you are wondering. If you painted me, you'd color me physical, spiritual, and emotional. Together those make the complete picture of who I really am."

She stared at him. "I'm sorry."

He walked to her chair and lifted her to her feet. He stood close enough to kiss her. "You've done more for my self-esteem in these few short days than anyone I've met in a lifetime." He took a step back. "This stuff needed to be said between us, though I didn't expect it so soon. But I hope we can keep going from here."

She nodded a yes, then leaned her head toward him. Warm lips brushed his cheek.

Oh, how tempting to "keep going from here," but instead he touched her cheek in response. "That was nice."

Daniel eased Marjorie back into her chair before returning to his seat.

He crammed the pencil between his teeth. His mouth needed a distraction.

9

Marjorie shuddered as uneasiness set in. Her clasped hands moistened as she rested them on her blue dress. The church scene before her should have felt familiar, but much to her chagrin, it felt foreign. Her lack of ease didn't come from the fact this wasn't the same Baptist church she'd gone to as a little girl. It came because she hadn't gone to church since she her eighteenth birthday. And she hadn't paid attention in church or read the Bible for years before that.

Marjorie sighed. Her newborn adulthood hadn't turned her into a trouble maker, but it had caused her to turn her disappointments and worries inward, offering no release. Sitting here on the pew, waiting for church to begin, she understood that not being a trouble maker was no substitute for being a practicing Christian.

But if I tighten my faith, I'll have to unravel my emotions.

Controlling those emotions had been her unwonted source of comfort for years.

She took in her surroundings. The sanctuary was packed with people. While parishioners settled into their places, chatter mixed with soft voices and good-to-see-yous moved throughout the aisles. Rain pattered against the stain glass windows in rhythm to the harmonies coming from the organ. She recognized the tune. The wooden pew stood strong against her back, as though it were promising to keep her steady.

Beside her, Tali Buckler's lemon scent teased her nose. Marjorie could hear Daniel's mother seated two people over rifling through her purse. A sniffle announced her need for a tissue. The poor woman had allergies, as Marjorie had learned in the week she'd dwelt in the Buckler home. Theo iterated to his father what foods he'd select at Ludy's Cafeteria for lunch today. The boy seemed to favor meats and dessert, for she'd not heard him list a vegetable.

What she'd been listening for were footsteps that stopped at their row. Daniel had yet to arrive from his Sunday School class. Maybe he wouldn't join his family on the pew. She wished she'd accepted his offer to go to class with him instead of with his folks. In a muddled effort to not appear as a girlfriend, she chose to sit in a Sunday School class of older married adults, obviously out of place.

Marjorie had no idea what her demeanor would be seeing him in church. Nor his, for that matter. How do two people who aren't a couple follow up in church after an admitted interest in one another? The attraction to him seemed shameful at church.

Maybe I'm over thinking it. How does God feel about these things?

Last Sunday morning she'd sat alone, studying at Valene's until Daniel came mid-afternoon and escorted her to his family's home. This week, when schedules had them both at Hillhurst, they'd kept up the guise of friendship, much like the week prior—a meal at the diner, a study session at the open library. And the Stewart conversation.

"Turns out I went to elementary school with Valene's brother who also works at Hillhurst."

"Interesting."

"Very. I'll tell you about it."

This week's one distinction from the week before was Fall Friday Chili Night around the Buckler table. Six nights into living with his family, Marjorie had already felt at ease. Mrs. Buckler had asked her to make cornbread, rummaging in a box for the recipe she'd likely memorized with years of cooking.

Marjorie smiled at a memory.

"Yahtzee," she exclaimed, around the table after supper. The family had battled one another for the coveted roll of dice in the game.

"What?" Daniel scooted his chair back and stood. He examined the dots on the white cubes with exaggerated motions before conceding the roll and giving her a wink before he sat back down.

Theo dubbed her the "Yahtzee Queen."

"Don't cross me, or its off with your head, Daniel Buckler." She slid a pencil toward him and chuckled.

She'd never played games with a family.

A bird chirped outside the stained-glass window. She shifted in the pew. Perhaps the most pressing question she had for herself was how a young woman who'd neglected her childhood faith could find her way back to it. Would she ever feel at home in church and in those silent moments between God and her? Maybe God wanted to fill the empty places left by the emotional pain she'd clung to so tightly. Was He waiting on her to make room?

Tali touched her arm and pointed. "See that girl in the brown dress? That's my best friend. She wants a manicure next time she comes over." The young lady displayed her own fingers and grinned. Joining Tali with a grin of her own, she nodded toward the best friend.

"That would be fun."

"What would be fun?" Daniel's voice made her jump.

With a "May I," and her approval, he maneuvered himself to sit next to Marjorie on the pew. Tali giggled. Marjorie moved a tad closer to the girl, making room for Daniel. "You look lovely. You had on this dress the first time I saw you," Daniel noted just as the organ signaled the service was starting.

Daniel sang the hymns with such passion that his few flat notes were no distraction. She sang too, her voice growing louder as she settled in to the once-familiar tunes. *I miss the comfort of this music.*

When the offering plate reached her, Marjorie dropped the five-dollar bill she'd pulled from her purse. Daniel's fingers grazed hers as the plate passed between them.

As the service progressed to the preaching, Daniel slid his open Bible to rest on his leg and hers, then pointed to the verse the pastor read. No need to open her own. He offered her a smile then his focus returned to the passage.

The man smelled good and looked like a dream in his blue suit and gray tie. Though at the moment, his apparent zeal for church was the most attractive thing about him. That truth caught her off guard, then his words came back to her. *If you painted who I am, you'd color me physical, spiritual, and emotional.* Mr. Daniel Buckler was the most spiritual male she'd ever met.

The words from the pulpit drew her attention. The preacher was explaining the meaning behind the names of God. His teaching made God seem personal and sounded practical. Most of her Bible learning had come from a Bible story shared in class. The few sermons she had heard growing up made the Bible difficult to comprehend. Maybe her childhood immaturity had skewed her opinion, but as a young woman sitting on the pew today, the words stirred her.

Her parents had never been there for her, yet had she not recognized that Jehovah Shammah, the Lord is There, had been present all along? That same God was Jehovah Roi, the God Who Sees Me, and had not neglected her. He'd watched her grow and even had a purpose for her. She'd felt it a few days ago in the shop while talking with Gordon and when washing Mr. Winkle's hair. If God was this personal and close, then perhaps she should risk her emotions and her life's truth with Him. Indeed, He already knew the truth about her.

• • •

When had she slipped her arm through Daniel's? Marjorie reckoned the gentle tension she'd felt when the preacher opened up the altar for responses triggered that motion. She was tense and felt a tug on her heart. She slid her arm away and noticed Daniel's gaze. His eyes watered. A gentle, inquiring smile formed on his lips. The man understood. Her body softened at the realization.

"I'm not ready to talk about it."

His smile now offered warmth and comfort, and she took it.

"But maybe soon." She released the words as though they were delicate glass.

"Anytime."

An odd mixture of regret and relief seeped through Marjorie as the service ended and folks began to scatter to form clusters of conversation. She stood with the Bucklers.

The tug at her heart lessened, but still remained. She recognized it for what it was—a pull toward setting things right with God.

Daniel nudged her arm and indicated Gordon and his family at the back of the sanctuary. He looked tall standing next to a petite wife, who hoisted a toddler on her hip. "I'll get his attention." Daniel's fragrance lingered as he ambled away.

"Don't move." Tali's eyes shone. "I'm gonna bring my friend here to meet you." Marjorie laughed. Mrs. Buckler watched her daughter saunter off. "She thinks you hung the moon." Marjorie improvised a response at the endearment. "Well, in that case, let's hope it's not fixin' to fall any minute now."

Locked into her spot on the aisle, Marjorie found herself surrounded by people who wanted to meet her. As she shook hands with every one of them, her eyes moistened. Had she ever felt so welcomed and loved before? Gordon approached and introduced his family to her and Mrs. Buckler.

"Does Valene come to church here?"

Gordon took the toddler from his wife. "No, she and Wanda attend the Methodist church."

The family bid their adieus.

Daniel and his father seemed focused on a conversation with a man she didn't know. Of course, she could count on two hands the people she knew in this congregation. Marjorie chuckled when she spotted Rusty standing next to the man. She'd met Rusty for certain.

Marjorie turned to Mrs. Buckler. "Do I have time for the ladies' room before we leave?" Lucy Buckler pointed. "Of course. It's in the foyer. Door on the left." She'd have to pass by the preacher and his wife enroute. Marjorie took a deep breath, then walked slowly toward the pastor, who stood at the foyer entrance. Her bladder protested the slow gait, but her nerves insisted.

What in the world should she say? Was there an etiquette she didn't know about? Her shoulders tensed. Perhaps the truth would be best. An it-was-nice-to-be-here might do. She paused in front of him, and the preacher spoke before she could part her lips. Of course—the man was a professional and a host. She stood in his house, after all—well, sorta.

"Nice to have you today."

"I enjoyed being here."

He introduced his wife, who then kept the conversation going.

"Are you related to the Bucklers?"

"Oh, no, ma'am. Actually, I just moved in with them. I'm renting their extra room."

"Wonderful. Then I hope to see you back, Miss..."

"Mullins. I'm Marjorie Mullins."

And just like that, the preacher's wife drew her into a conversation. Before she excused herself—now she really had to go to the bathroom—the couple knew she grew up then worked at Anderson and was now attending beauty school and working at The Wright Do. The only thing she hadn't confessed were her sins. Though in reality, the pair likely cared about her spiritual story even more than what she'd just shared with them. And they likely knew the answer to her earlier pondering about attraction. *Maybe the Bible has the answer, and I won't have to ask someone.*

Excusing herself, she entered the foyer and opened the door to the ladies' room. Being alone in there for a moment calmed the nerves she didn't know she'd had.

Ready to depart, Marjorie stepped toward one of the sinks as another woman opened the restroom door and went directly to the opposite sink. The blond woman leaned over and moaned, then turned on the faucet. Marjorie didn't want to stare or impose, but here she stood unnoticed and feeling awkward. Oh well. She washed her hands, then pulled on the revolving white towel in the holder attached to the wall and dried her hands. The lady pulled a tissue from her purse and patted her face. When she looked up, Marjorie felt her mouth drop.

"Candace?"

The woman startled and stared with no apparent recollection of their prior meeting. And of course, probably clueless of the tangled web between them.

"I met you at the leasing office."

"Oh. Yes. I remember now." The woman tossed her tissue into the waste can.

"Are you alright?" Marjorie asked with concern.

"My stomach is upset."

"Something you ate?"

"Something." The woman smiled then seemed to morph her composure into the confident woman with the "fall in love, and pay the price" demeanor. Her pale face denied the pretense. She held the door as Marjorie walked through. "Did you find a place to live?"

"She did."

Marjorie jumped at Daniel's reply. The man stood in the foyer.

"Daniel. How do you two know each other?"

Speaking of upset stomachs, Marjorie wanted to puke at the sultry way Candace pronounced his name then drawled out her question.

Marjorie blurted before Daniel could reply. "From Hillhurst. I work at The Wright Do."

How would he handle the awkward situation? As for herself, should she play ignorant over knowing Candace and Daniel had been a couple?

And while she was at it, should she screech like a mad woman and declare Daniel her own? Well, ok, her own friend because she'd demanded that. Probably not worth a conniption fit.

The man himself filled the gap.

"Candace, this is Marjorie Mullins."

"We met at the leasing office. Which is why I asked if she found a place to live. Which you answered, 'she did.'" The woman paused. "You two must talk a lot at work." The air seemed to chill with the remark. "What did you find, Marjorie?"

"I'm renting a room with a family." *Daniel's family.*

The man looked at Candace. "Decided to come to this church instead of the one with your parents?" Marjorie hitched a breath at the sarcasm in Daniel's voice.

"I thought the change would be good."

"Oh, is that right?" Daniel's hand pressed against Marjorie's back. "We best get going. My folks already left for the cafeteria." With that, he edged her forward and tucked her hand into his arm.

Candace didn't look as charming with her mouth hanging open.

Marjorie rubbed her thumb on Daniel's suit coat. Nice.

. . .

Ludy's Cafeteria in downtown Hazel bustled with activity on Sundays. The place was large, and one of the few eateries open to accommodate hungry churchgoers. The long line moved quickly as patrons made their selections, which servers dished onto a plastic tray with compartments. That part of the dining experience reminded Daniel of the school cafeteria.

He pushed the rest of his fried chicken to the edge of his plate. His appetite had waned earlier—the moment he saw Candace and Marjorie enter the foyer together. Nerves had taken over. In fact, the buffet combination of aromas from practically every food on the planet nauseated him right now.

His universes had collided for a second when he saw the two of them emerge Then he was struck by what the eyes of his heart noticed. The beautiful, ebony-haired Marjorie resembled a portrait rich with color and textures. She captivated his gaze. Candace appeared no more than a child's crayon drawing that solicited a polite nod.

The truth hit him. He hadn't survived an agony the day his fiancée had walked off. He'd been spared one.

Looking across the table at Marjorie, engaged in conversation with his mother, as ridiculous as it seemed, Daniel wanted to drop to one knee slap dab in the middle of the cafeteria and ask her to marry him.

Yet, he'd take his time. He understood her concern that he had so-called loved another woman. In time, she'd come to understand, as he had, that he'd never been in love until the day Curtis pushed Rusty into the woman wearing a blue dress.

Why in the world had Candace shown up at his church today? She'd been absent for weeks, and now she'd appeared the day after calling him at home. Suspicion set in that there was a motive to her timing.

"Stop." He stilled his shaking leg beneath the table.

"What'd you say, Daniel?"

He turned to Theo on his left. "Nuthin'. Here," he slid his plate toward his brother, "want my drumstick?"

"Uh huh. And, you said something." Theo pointed a finger at each ear. "These things are top notch."

Daniel laughed. "Then why'd you need me to repeat it?"

The boy shrugged a shoulder, then sunk his teeth into the drumstick. "Miss Marjorie, I can't deal with him anymore. Mind taking over?" The words were squished into dark meat.

"He drives me bonkers too, Theo." A shoe nudged his shin and Daniel's knee hit the table. "Hey, that hurt." He enjoyed their interaction.

An image of kissing Marjorie teased him. Daniel stilled his mind. He intended his first real kiss with Marjorie to prove nothing but his love for her.

Yep, he loved her. He didn't care how much time had or hadn't passed between them.

How had he ever thought he fell in love with Candace?

Motion behind him shook Daniel from his thoughts. Valene approached the table with Wanda at her side. He stood.

"Wanda, it's good to see you. I'm glad you're feeling better."

"For the most part." The woman surveyed the table.

"Folks, this is Mrs. Darden. She's one of my art students. You likely recognize her name from the story on Troy Darden, her son. Wanda, this is my family. And of course, you know Marjorie from the shop."

His family uttered polite hellos and condolences.

Wanda eyed Marjorie. "I thought you didn't have a family."

Daniel jaws tensed.

"Wanda, she's renting a room at the Buckler home." Valene explained.

"And she already feels like family." Lucy Buckler to the rescue. Daniel eyed his mother and smiled.

"The Bucklers have been very gracious. You look lovely in that color, Mrs. Darden." Marjorie interjected.

Daniel beamed at both her composure and her observation. Never once had he considered Wanda Darden to look lovely, yet standing before him, he saw her with his artist's eyes. The power of color to transform an object amazed him.

"Well, Marjorie is already an asset to our shop." Valene placed her hand on Marjorie's shoulder. The woman was honorable. Daniel's appreciation for her grew.

Goodbyes were spoken and his family rose to leave. As Daniel pulled out Marjorie's chair, a familiar figure edged past him holding a bowl of orange gelatin. Recognition set in.

"Curtis."

The boy turned; his own awareness obvious. He drew his arm behind him as though hiding the dessert. Daniel stifled a laugh. Orange gelatin must not be cool enough by the boy's peer pressure standards.

"Hey."

"How'd your game go?"

"We won."

Curtis' eyes locked onto Tali, and Daniel grimaced. Seeming to notice the stare, his dad slid his arm around his daughter's shoulder.

The boy's eyes then flitted to Marjorie, and he offered Daniel a wry smile before walking away.

. . .

"Thanks for taking a ride with me before I drop you off."

"I've never seen this side of town."

Daniel rested a hand on the console while the other maneuvered the car down Elm Lane. Like the woman sitting next to him, the street was a sight to behold. Why he'd never painted it, he wasn't sure. He'd have to do that one day. *But not until I paint Marjorie.* The oldest and most stately homes in town claimed Elm Lane as an address. Large elm trees lined each side of the road, their branches meeting in the middle to form a green canopy.

Daniel had chosen this peaceful route for a reason, hoping to soothe his edginess. As he took in the soothing sight and calm spread, dadgum, his appetite returned. Too bad he'd given that drumstick to Theo.

"I just want to remind you that Candace means nothing to me. I have no idea why she showed up at church today."

"She didn't go to that church before?"

"No, other than when we were engaged."

"She's still in love with you, Daniel."

"No, she's not."

"I disagree."

"She's not in love, but I don't doubt she's up to something."

"You seem certain of both." Marjorie twisted her watch band.

"I am. My gut tells me that's the case, and I can't shake the feeling. Did I tell you her husband, or ex-husband, whatever he is, called me a few days ago?"

"What for?"

127

"To explain what happened between them. Then and now. When I said I wasn't interested, he hung up." His heart thumped at her slight grin.

"Well, my gut says she wants your attention."

Do you?

He slowed the car to a stop. "I don't want her attention, and I don't love her." He leaned over and rested his forehead against Marjorie's. "I want to get to know you. And, I think..."

He'd better keep those other three words to himself for now.

He pecked the cheek of his friend, turned up the radio, and hit the gas.

Marjorie's mouth hung open ever so slightly.

"Might want to close those lips, or bugs will get in."

An elbow nudged his arm. "You really do drive me bonkers."

Fair enough, seeing she made him crazy.

• • •

Daniel looked out over the heads of his students, scribbling away at their tests. Most Mondays there was no place he'd rather be, but not today. He shook his head to clear the funk, but it didn't go anywhere.

He was twenty-four years old and wanted to redeem the time his relationship with Candace had wasted. He stood and moved down a row between the desks. If they knew how distracted he was, the talkers and few cheaters would take full advantage. The afternoon sun slipped through the blinds, creating lines across the classroom that bathed some students in ideal light. He smiled at the sight.

He hadn't known Marjorie existed when he'd been with Candace, so what would he be redeeming anyway? He stilled. The answer was his own judgment. He'd think more highly of himself if he'd recognized Candace's phony loyalty early on and his own lack of love for her. Perhaps, like the sun coming through the window, his heart had bathed her in the best light. After the jilting, Candace morphed into a sadness that tinted his life. Upon her return, she'd become a heaviness he couldn't seem to shake, no matter how much his thoughts went to Marjorie. No matter how awestruck he felt in her presence.

Daniel turned down another row, and one of his paintings caught his eye. He paused. Man, getting texture and details of the pecan tree just right had taken a lot of effort. It had been worth it though. The scene depicted such an ordinary sight in this part of Texas—pecans lying scattered at the base of the tree trunk. Some would be gathered. Others would be trampled. Yet, his eye had seen more. The pecan tree stood as an emblem of productivity, effort, and life beyond one's self. He'd been a week from college graduation when he sat on campus and painted the tree beside his dorm. He'd felt inspired and excited to contribute to the world and young lives. The painting hung in his classroom because of that inspiration.

He returned his focus back to those he meant to inspire. He'd see Marjorie soon and could think on her all he wanted this evening. He bent and grabbed an eraser from the floor. If only Candace were a mistaken answer on a test that he could erase and replace.

One by one, students came and placed the finished tests on the corner of his desk. It was the last period of the day, so those who finished early were allowed to doodle on sketch paper he kept on a shelf. "You have twenty minutes left." His stroll through the aisles wound down.

When the last test was placed on his desk, Daniel raised his right arm, the signal permitting talking and moving around the classroom before the bell rang. Students never knew when he'd use it, but they did know the aisles, desks, and pupils had to be orderly, and all work completed before he'd grant the freedom.

Daniel dared not turn his back on the class when he granted freedom, so he loosened his tie, leaned against his desk, legs and arms crossed, and observed the social dynamics displayed before him.

Curtis approached him. How had he pulled himself away from the girls who'd flocked him? Even more intriguing was why?

"Mr. Buckler, are you dating that orphan lady I saw you with?"

Daniel clenched his teeth. "That is rude, Curtis. My dating life is not your concern." *And who told you Marjorie was an orphan?*

"She's pretty, but I wondered why you'd date an orphan?"

"What makes you think my friend is an orphan?" Daniel was adamant to find out how the news had spread.

"Rusty told me. At the cafeteria yesterday."

"You talked to Rusty at Ludy's?" Daniel hadn't seen Rusty and his family there.

"Our dads go to the same lodge, so we stopped at their table when we saw them. Rusty said he's your neighbor and knows all about her 'cause his mom talked to Mrs. Buckler."

Daniel glanced at the young man who'd been deemed a misfit. As suspected, he lingered on the outside of a group of boys who likely paid him no mind. Apparently, the young man had dangled his one bit of leverage in the social pool to get a nibble out of Curtis.

"Whether I am dating a woman or not, setting her apart as an orphan is rude and irrelevant." Did Curtis even know what that word meant?

"I think being an orphan is embarrassing."

"Being rude is embarrassing."

The bell rang, and Curtis vanished, leaving a hint of school pizza and Phys Ed class behind him. Did the girls not smell that?

"Rusty," Daniel called to the boy as he lumbered past him, "wait one second."

"I'll miss my bus."

"No, you won't."

Rusty paused.

"Did you tell Curtis that Miss Mullins is an orphan?"

The boy's face flushed. "Yes sir." He looked away.

"I just wondered. You're dismissed."

Rusty scurried through the doorway with a speed uncharacteristic of his usual gait. Daniel glanced at his watch, relieved the boy shouldn't miss the bus on his account.

In the teacher lounge, ten minutes later, he hoped the freshly brewed coffee shooed away his end-of-day fatigue while the dance committee chairwoman droned on and on. What he lacked in enthusiasm for the committee's tasks, she more than made up for. Daniel smirked. No wonder she coached the cheerleading squad. If the rules allowed, she'd probably dress out and cheer with her squad during the football games.

"So, the local beauty school offers discount prices. We need to have fliers made to advertise that so students know they have an affordable place for hair-dos."

"I may have another idea." *What made me say that?* "Why not see if they would offer a free nail thing-a-ma-jig with a hairdo? Manicure—that's what I meant. And an added discount for the boy haircuts in exchange for an ad in the yearbook?"

I may never live this suggestion down.

"That's a good idea. Do you still oversee the yearbook?"

"No, but I'll talk to Gerald Jones, who does."

"Great. I've got you down to talk to Gerald and to the college." He opened his mouth to protest about calling the college but realized he didn't mind one bit talking to Marjorie about his idea and then talking to the school.

"No guarantees." He fake-checked his watch. "I gotta scat."

And scat he did in his convertible. He entered the art classroom in the shadow of the last arrival.

"You're late." Wanda Darden cast him a frown from her seat at the front.

"On time." He grinned at her. He'd missed her when she was sick. Yet, she'd insulted Marjorie at the restaurant yesterday, and well, he didn't like that one bit. "Good to have you back in class, Wanda."

He marched toward the front and uncovered the painting he'd left Saturday. The art students followed suit with their own easels and began to paint. Daniel turned on the record player. Soon the motion of gentle strokes, the appealing scent of paint, and the rhythm of the music transitioned him from the teacher, to Daniel, the artist—although slightly distracted that Marjorie worked a hallway over. *Does she sense my nearness?*

"Daniel?" He turned to find Wanda looking at him. He made his way to her.

Instinct made him glance at her work. "Wanda, those narrow strokes are excellent."

"Thank you. Tell me, are you dating that Marjorie girl?

You mean woman? And what's with the word "that?" And what is this—pry-into-my- business—day? Bad-mouth-Marjorie day? Are Curtis and Wanda in cahoots somehow? Impossible. He lassoed the thoughts before they emerged as words.

"We are friends."

Wanda smirked. "I may be old, but I fell in love once. I saw how you eyed her yesterday."

"I'd be happy if the friendship grew into more." No need for Wanda to know details.

"She seems sweet enough, but she probably has a past."

"That's rude and absurd to say."

"What I mean is, she's an orphan. Something happened in her past."

"Yeah, she was born, was placed in a home, and grew into a phenomenal woman. That's her past."

"There was likely a scandal with her parents."

"Or a death." Regret seized him as Wanda's face paled. "How callous of me to say, Wanda."

The woman blinked her eyes and exhaled. "Perhaps, but my words were no better."

"Do you think poorly of Marjorie?"

"No. I suppose you think I do. Truth is, I relate to her being without family. And that makes me uncomfortable."

She used the word "uncomfortable," but Daniel sensed a more accurate descriptor such as "intimidated." Did Marjorie's potential, despite her past, seem a threat to Wanda's life achievements and place in the community? Did she worry that she would out-do her in talent and fortitude? The workings of a woman's mind baffled him.

"So, instead of painting Marjorie in a bad light, how about you focus on her talents and potential? Paint her for the person God has gifted her to be."

"You speak like a poet, Daniel."

"Or an artist."

"Or a man in love." Wanda turned and faced her canvas.

10

Marjorie wished she could toss herself into the washer with the towels. She heard Stewart's high, thin voice on the other side of the break room door. This would be his third attempt today to corner her in the shop. His nonchalance appeared pathetically obvious. And Valene was either oblivious or hopeful over his attempts. She certainly didn't seem bothered.

"Here, sis, I'll take that dirty wash rag."

Great! In her haste to bunker at the washing machine, she'd overlooked a dirty cloth.

The door opened, and Stewart's body filled the doorway. She sucked in a breath.

"One more for the load." He entered and the door shut behind him.

Ugh.

Stewart extended the wash rag to her, and Marjorie pinched a corner of it between her fingers, careful to avoid any contact with his hand. She tossed it onto the floor.

"Both our shifts are over in an hour. Would you like to join me for supper?"

"No, thanks. I've got homework tonight, and don't you remember..."

"I remember I said I'd take you out when I got back in town. I'm back."

Marjorie huffed.

"You can pick the place."

I can also pick the man, and it's not you. "That's not the point. Stewart, I was going to remind you that I'm not interested in you romantically."

"Or at all, it seems."

Well said, but she wouldn't express her agreement aloud. The noise of the agitating washer pretty much summed up her emotions over Stewart.

"It's fine to be acquaintances at work. Nothing else. I'm not trying to be rude. Just honest."

"Honest, aye? Daniel Buckler was a night away from marrying that Candace. I hear she's back in town. A man doesn't forget his first love. I speak from experience." He pointed between them. *Was that supposed to be a joke?* Her stomach churned. "So, I wouldn't set my sights on him if I were you."

"That's your unsolicited opinion and none of your business."

He smiled. "Acquaintances for now." He left the room.

Marjorie slumped into the chair, banging her elbow against the table. "Ouch." Her insides quivered. The man had voiced her greatest fear about the good-looking teacher.

The washer stopped. She quickly soaped the wash rag and cleaned it by hand, then loaded it and the towels into the dryer. How fortunate that Valene had the latest front load models of washer and dryer in the shop. Running wet towels through a ringer and hanging them to dry would take twice the time. She'd done plenty of that type laundering at the orphanage. Miss Bords had thrown a hot chocolate party the night a donor brought in two sets of automatic washers and dryers. "It's okay if you spill a drop on your clothes," she'd joked. Marjorie smiled at the memory. The evening was one of the only times she'd seen the matron relaxed outside of listening to college football.

A tenderness took Marjorie by surprise. Had Miss Bords settled in to her new home and job? She ought to write and tell her how school and work were going. In reply, Miss Bords would likely ask if she'd opened the envelope.

She ought to open it.

Yesterday's sermon had taken residence in her mind. Could she handle whatever news the envelope held if she clung to God, the Father? Daniel would probably say yes, with certainty.

She glanced at her watch. Thirty minutes and she'd be free. And so would Stewart. The man would likely make a fourth attempt at her today. She'd flee as soon as she folded the last towel. No meandering to Daniel's art room. No waiting around for him. Surely if she didn't go to him, he'd come looking for her.

She'd leave word that she had to scurry home and would see him later.

And she'd hope, hope, hope, that he'd take the hint and show up at his parent's house tonight.

She'd kick herself if he didn't, though she'd much rather kick Stewart.

. . .

As the art students cleaned up their areas, Daniel walked to the back of the classroom one more time and glanced down the hallway.

He checked his watch. Was Marjorie not coming to meet him? Was he being foolish to assume she would? Maybe she'd gotten detained. He'd hurry to the shop and wait for her. He grinned. He'd gone almost twenty-four hours without seeing her, and now he waited like a puppy, eager for interaction.

At the tap on his shoulder, Daniel turned to face Wanda Darden.

"Would you mind walking me to the dining room? I'm a bit tired."

The request seemed uncharacteristic of the Wanda he'd come to know. "Sure. Let me grab my things." At least, if Marjorie were headed his way, they'd pass each other in the hall.

Wanda slid her arm through his when he offered the support. The scent of her elixir reminded him of his step-mother. If Wanda weren't moving at such a slow pace, he'd be suspicious of her request to be escorted, assuming she had more opinion to express. But there was no denying the woman felt weary. Daniel glanced at her. If he were to paint her now, he'd paint an aged and weary woman seeping through the coiffured hair and make-up.

"Your Marjorie is very talented in the salon. I can spot talent."

He chuckled. "My Marjorie?"

Wanda patted his arm where her hand rested. "The point is, she's very talented from what Valene says and my own observations."

"That's high praise coming from a professional like yourself."

It was Wanda's time to chuckle. "If you say so."

"Marjorie might appreciate hearing that from you."

"Now, don't push me, Daniel. I have a reputation to uphold."

"I see that you're a real softy, Mrs. Darden. But don't worry, I won't spread the word."

They continued in silence, and as they reached the dining room, the smell of fried chicken made his stomach growl. Wanda pulled him to an abrupt stop.

"I can't go in there. I think I'm going to be sick. Take me to my room."

Daniel made an about-face toward the residential hall. Wanda leaned into him. They weren't going to make it far before she passed out or threw up. He was unprepared for both.

A figure dressed in white turned onto the hallway ahead of him. "Hey! A little help here." Daniel heard the panic in his own voice. The man trotted toward them.

"Mrs. Darden is sick."

The man took Wanda's other arm and tucked it inside his own. Daniel felt the burden of Mrs. Darden's body lessen.

"I need the clinic, Stewart." Wanda whispered, and Daniel's stomach dropped. He'd never heard her sound so weak.

Daniel glanced at the attendant, who indicated to take a right at the connecting hall. Had Wanda been this sick in the class-room, and he'd not noticed? He'd have to be more alert to eye his senior students. They may not pass notes or sneak gum like the junior-highers, but he realized now that an ailment could sneak up on them.

Daniel released Mrs. Darden to a nurse who took over his role.

"You get better, Wanda. I'll pray for you." He touched the woman's arm as he spoke. She offered a thin smile.

"Thanks, man." The attendant spoke over his shoulder.

"Glad you came along." Daniel pivoted toward the door then paused.

Stewart.

This had to be the man from elementary school Marjorie had told him about.

He looked around him. Oh, man, he'd likely missed her with the diversion—if she'd come to meet him.

He hoofed it to the shop and found Gordon spraying the hair of a lone patron.

"Marjorie still here?"

"She left lickety-split. Said she had homework. Said to tell you she'd see you later."

His shoulders drooped. Gordon laughed. "You got it bad." The patron in the chair giggled.

Daniel wasn't much in the mood for humor.

"She made sure I didn't forget to tell you 'She'd. See. You. Later,'" Gordon reiterated.

The man had made his point. Marjorie hoped to see him.

Daniel whistled. "Yeah, man, I got it bad. And that's between the three of us." He tilted his head toward the client, Shoug—the pie lady. "Understood, Mrs. Jennings?" She mimicked zipping her lips shut.

"Is Valene still here?"

"In the supply room."

"Thanks."

He tapped on the supply room with his knuckle and pushed it open. Valene looked up from her tiny desk.

"I thought you'd want to know that Wanda left my art class sick. She's in the clinic."

Valene slumped her face into her hands and shook her head back and forth.

"Are you alright?" Daniel stepped inside the room.

Valene faced him. "I think something is terribly wrong with Wanda."

Daniel's thoughts jammed. He didn't know how to respond. "I hope not. I'll be praying for her."

Valene's thanks and shooing away were simultaneous, for which Daniel felt grateful, despite his concern.

He had somewhere to be and someone to see.

. . .

"Mom, I'm home." Daniel teased as he closed his parents' front door behind him. He'd frequented their home more often with Marjorie living there.

"What a surprise." His step-mother stood in the kitchen door-way. "I'll set another plate at the dining room table." She tapped her forehead. "Wait, I already did. Mother's intuition."

Daniel met her in the doorway and gave her a hug. He inhaled, hoping to catch the aroma of cooking food, but smelled none. Curious, he glanced at the stove but then spotted the object of his romantic affection sitting with Tali on the barstools at the high counter. Marjorie bit her lip, then grinned, while Tali hopped down to meet him with a hug. He'd prefer the flipped response.

"I'm helping Marjorie with her homework."

"Is that so?"

"Come see."

"What brings you here, Mr. Buckler?"

"Marjorie, don't be silly. It's Mom's cooking." Tali wiggled her eyebrows.

His step-mother laughed. "Not tonight. Your Dad is bringing home one of those chicken meals from the new restaurant. I'm finishing up the dessert."

Daniel glanced at the counter and laughed along with her. Lucy Buckler must have succumbed to a busy day, for on the counter lay a boxed frozen pie.

"I came here because I got some kind of covert message that I thought led me here." He moved to stand beside Marjorie. Tali hopped back up on her barstool.

"Is that so?" Marjorie continued to pore over the textbook in front of her. "Wherever could that covert message have come from, I wonder?" She looked up with a saucy grin.

His heart flip-flopped. Tearing his gaze from hers and his thoughts from where they wanted to go, he looked down at the drawings of the human head divided into sections on the page she studied.

"What's this?" He spoke over Marjorie's shoulder. Man, she smelled delicious.

"I'm learning how to divide the hair into sections to cut or style."

"And that?" He pointed to drawings of women's faces.

"Those are types of facial structure. I have to know that so I can give the haircut and hair do that makes my clients look their best."

"And I thought a comb and some cream were all I needed for perfection."

Marjorie elbowed him.

"Seriously, that's impressive, Miss Mullins."

His fingers lifted her chin while his eyes scanned her face. He glanced at the drawings in the book. "I'd say you're heart-shaped." He winked. Her blush warmed his insides.

"That's what I think too." She winked in return.

"I'm oval-shaped." Oh, right, Tali was in the room. He turned and examined his sister's features with his fingers. "Sho' 'nuff. The purdiest oval in Texas."

Marjorie laughed. "That's an awful Texas drawl for a true Texan."

"And, what's this?" Daniel pointed to two Styrofoam models of a head and face resting next to the textbook.

Marjorie explained the practice dummies, and an idea struck him.

"So, are those yours? Like, do you get to keep them?"

"Yes. Why?"

"That's for after supper." Along with his other idea about the dance dos.

When the rest of the family retired to the living room with filled bellies, Daniel joined Marjorie and her sidekick Tali at the small kitchen table. He propped his art bag beside his chair.

"So, how about I draw those lines on the skulls of your dummies?" He suddenly felt ridiculous. "That is, if it will be helpful."

Marjorie's face lit up. "That's a great idea. But can you do it with something that won't rub off? I have to put practice wigs on these."

"I've got permanent markers in my bag."

"Dandy!" She handed him one of the heads and turned the open book toward him.

Daniel worked while Marjorie pinned a wig on the other sculpture and ratted the hair with a rat tail comb. Daniel smiled. The black comb with a slender, metal tail had an awful name. Tali drew various hairstyles on a sketch pad. The girl was an artist in her own right.

"Tali," her mom called from the other room, "our show is on."

His sister jumped from the table. "You guys coming?"

"Not tonight. We've got work to do." Daniel spoke through the pencil in his mouth. When had he stuck it there? He yanked it out and tossed it into his art bag. He glanced at Marjorie who mouthed her thanks.

Tali came around the corner of the table and paused at Daniel's work. Not only had he drawn the dotted lines, but he'd begun drawing blue eyes. Below the eyes lay red lips. A slim, petite nose filled the space in between. Tali put her hand over her mouth, surprising him with her discretion. She'd recognized the face of Marjorie coming to life on the model.

When Tali left the kitchen, Daniel tapped Marjorie's shoe with his own.

"She bothering you at all?"

"She's adorable. I like having her around." She blushed. "But, just chatting with you is nice too. I'm sorry I skedaddled from the shop. I was avoiding Stewart. Not you." She explained the encounters.

Daniel filled Marjorie in on his day, omitting all references about her being an orphan and ending with his own Stewart encounter. "But Wanda seemed to get sick so fast. Valene is worried something is bad wrong."

"Poor woman. She's ornery, but somehow, I really like her. Isn't that crazy? I like her, but she intimidates me to death."

"I heard it from the woman herself that she thinks you're talented."

Marjorie's eyes brightened. "Tell me."

"I just did."

"Details, Daniel. I need word-for-word what she said."

He wasn't sure he remembered every word, but he gave Marjorie enough to satisfy her.

"Do you have a black wig in that bag of yours?"

"Yes."

"Can I borrow it right quick? I won't mess it up."

Marjorie's face wrinkled with question, but she reached into the bag and unwound a mass of black hair— or something like hair. He took it and placed it on the mannequin head.

"What are you doing?" Marjorie tried to get up to see.

"Stay put. It's a surprise. Look at me and don't wiggle."

Marjorie laughed.

"Be still." He laughed in return, then ran his fingers through the mass of black hair, making an attempt to flip up the ends. He'd always thought his artist hands dexterous and kind of refined, but working through the mass, they felt bulky and awkward.

He sat back in his chair. "Ok. Close your eyes." She complied and he turned the mannequin head toward her. "Open them."

Marjorie gasped. "It's me."

"Yes."

"Daniel, that's amazing. You make me look so good."

"God made you look so good—I say that with respect. Now, who do you want this next one to be?"

"You!"

"No way! You're not putting lady hair on my head."

Marjorie pushed back her chair and came to stand beside him. She took his hands. "You're such a good artist." He rubbed her fingers with his thumb. She slipped free and returned to her chair. "Why don't you make it look like Tali. I think she'd like that."

"Can you swap heads?" He burst out laughing. "I sound like a junior high kid."

They swapped mannequins, and Marjorie removed the black wig, studying the dotted segments he'd drawn for her. They worked in silence until he noticed Marjorie yawn.

"You're tired, and I hear the show going off the air."

"Big day tomorrow. I hope I pass the hair section test tomorrow."

"I think you will. Got time for me to run an idea by you?"

Marjorie gave him her full attention as he shared his idea about the beauty school.

"I bet the administrator might like that. I can talk to her for you, if you don't mind."

"That's nice of you. No pressure to do that tomorrow. You've got a test to think about."

"Now you sound like a junior high *teacher*, Mr. Buckler."

They both packed up, and Daniel stood to pull out her chair. He fought to keep his composure as the undeniable draw between them made him want to pull her close. He sought to see the same struggle in her eyes, but the boldness taking his hands had vanished, as she kept her eyes downcast and her thoughts concealed.

Daniel went to tell his family goodbye, then headed outside. He grinned when Marjorie followed. They stood at his car door.

"Daniel, I've been thinking. I've decided to open the envelope."

Wow. He hadn't expected that. "That's brave of you."

"The truth is, I've yearned to know all along. It could be helpful to know. I was just determined not to. I'm not sure when I'll do it, but soon."

She stood before him both vulnerable and courageous.

Their eyes locked, and Daniel pulled her into an embrace.

"Thank you, Daniel."

His hand swept over her hair.

"Marjorie, I'm not a saint. We better part ways."

"If you're feeling like I am, then yes, get out of here. This is feeling like more than friendship"

"Far more." He brushed his hand over her soft hair again.

He hopped over the closed door, thankful he'd left the top down, and started the car. Within moments, the night air chilled his skin, though his insides were still flaming.

Moments from home, Daniel finally felt settled inside and out. The fact that Marjorie planned to open the envelope was a big deal. And in his mind, a step toward her coming to terms with herself. "Help her, God."

If she'd have him, he'd marry her one day, no matter if the news of her past wounded or encouraged her. He hoped and prayed she'd be better for it. After all, her mother cared enough to leave her an explanation.

Daniel leaned forward and blinked. A car sat in front of his house. As he turned on his blinker, he saw the driver toss a cigarette out the window. He turned into his driveway and watched the figure emerge.

Candace.

If he shoved the car into reverse and barreled out the drive, he'd run over her. An injured ex-fiancée would not bode well for him. He stayed put.

"What are you doing here, Candace?"

"I've been waiting for you since school let out. I need to talk to you."

"Are you in danger?"

"Don't be silly. I'm being serious."

"I'm being serious too. Are you in danger?"

"No."

"Then go ahead and get back in your car and drive off. I'm not the person you should talk to anymore. You are or were another man's wife."

"We know each other so well, and I need someone who would understand my dilemma."

"You don't know me well at all. Not anymore. Does this dilemma put you in danger?"

"No."

"So, Candace, find someone else to talk with."

She huffed and returned to her car. When her tail lights were out of sight, he walked over and opened the garage door.

Her words pounded his brain. "I've been waiting for you since school was out." That action felt obnoxious. He spit on the ground. He would not let her rile him like she had when she called him. Not only had she begun to repulse him emotionally, she now looked unattractive. Candace appeared puny, tired, and reeked of cigarette smoke. Her once pleasing presence now felt possessive. Any semblance of kindness she'd had in the past seemed to have given way to selfishness. "Thank you, God." He'd been spared the horror of waking up each morning to someone he'd come to dislike.

Daniel parked the car in the garage and made his way inside the house. He looked out the large, kitchen window. Would she dare come back? He paced to the refrigerator, chugging the last of the orange juice. His stomach rebelled. He double checked the locks of every window and door before heading for bed.

"Get yourself together." The man in the bathroom mirror stared back with pursed lips. "Candace is acting wacky, but she's not a stalker." The reflection smirked then wrinkled his brow.

But, what in the world could possess the woman to sit outside his house for hours?

11

Aisle twelve would likely prove to be her favorite. Marjorie pushed the shopping cart at a leisurely pace, though her heart raced with excitement. She didn't want to overlook any of the cookie and baking options available to her. She supposed grocery shopping was a mundane task for many women. A chore. Yet, in her opinion, weaving through the aisles was an adventure. Cleaning community toilets at the orphanage qualified as a chore.

The store teemed with movement. A stream of shoppers flew past her. Some wrestled with children hanging on their buggy or grabbing for items that apparently weren't on the list. Others reached for items with extreme precision, in a ritualistic fashion. Marjorie grinned. If her childlike wonder shone, no one noticed, each focused on the task at hand or on the shopper huddled with them sharing news in hushed tones. Would the community of patrons be surprised to learn this was her first time to shop in a grocery store?

She paused to read the instructions for frosted brownies printed on a tin of cocoa. Feeling confident she could measure, stir, and pour, then measure, mix, and spread, she placed the brown tin in her buggy. No doubt Mrs. Buckler had all the listed ingredients in her kitchen, but Marjorie wanted these baked treats to be an offering of appreciation to her hosting family, so she'd pick up everything. She rolled further down the aisle toward the flour, flinching as an approaching buggy squeaked. An employee with a high voice announced the day's special—golden ripe bananas, eight cents a pound.

Mrs. Buckler had said she could use the kitchen anytime. Marjorie bounced on her toes. She could also make a batch of brownies to take to Valene and Daniel to thank them for their investment in her. Satisfaction covered her like a warm blanket.

Daniel's eyes had watered when she told him about her plan for the envelope. She'd never forget that image. Life had given her limited encounters with men. The occasional interaction with a male teacher, custodian, or physician did not qualify for knowing someone. Daniel was becoming her first meaningful male friendship, romantic or otherwise.

"Pardon me." A woman reached around her and picked up a bag of flour. Marjorie excused herself and smiled at the woman. In return, the shopper offered a slight head nod, while simultaneously telling her young daughter, "No, you cannot have any more animal crackers." Marjorie chuckled when she saw the child's cheeks stuffed like a chipmunk. A small opened box of the crackers hung from a string on the child's arm.

Marjorie imagined her own future in the scene. One day.

She moved forward, pausing at the vanilla. Wondering what the differences were between imitation and pure, she shrugged her shoulder and reached for the less expensive one.

"I'd suggest you choose the pure for better flavor."

She jumped and turned toward the voice. Valene stood before her, with Mrs. Darden at her side.

Marjorie grabbed the bottle of pure vanilla. "Hello! I need all the help I can get with these brownies. I'm not an experienced baker."

"The secret is to not over stir the batter." Mrs. Darden's face gave no hint of feeling ill nor of being rude. In fact, her eyes shone bright and friendly. Marjorie fought the urge to lean closer in and examine the pupils.

"Thanks. I'll remember that."

"You can mix hair color, so you can certainly mix brownies." Mrs. Darden smiled.

Marjorie clamped her mouth shut to make sure it didn't gape open at the compliment. She'd rather be showing a big smile on her face like Valene. Something stirred in Marjorie's heart. Here stood Mrs. Darden, without a family of her own. The orphan in her could not ignore the connection between herself and this lady who also rattled her nerves.

"Are you feeling better, Mrs. Darden? Daniel told me you were sick."

"I am."

Valene rubbed the lady's arm. "We're gonna get her to the hospital for some tests. Maybe they can see what is causing these attacks."

"I hope so."

Like the huddles Marjorie had observed up and down the aisles, the three of them stood and chatted. Marjorie shared about her day at beauty school and her success on the test. At last, she shared the good news she hadn't yet been able to tell Daniel. The beauty school would partner with the junior high to provide a blocked time and special discounts for their students. In return, they'd get a free ad in the yearbook. Marjorie had even been tasked to inquire with the high school about a similar arrangement.

"That's a splendid idea." Wanda's face seemed to light up.

"Daniel had the idea. I simply asked the administrator."

"I like that young man." Wanda's cheeks blushed beneath her overstated rouge.

Me too. Marjorie grinned. "He's a good person."

This inside-out demeanor of Wanda perplexed Marjorie. Is this the side Daniel had witnessed? Marjorie sighed inwardly and let the woman's kindness wash over her.

When the trio split up, Marjorie steered her cart toward the dairy section for eggs and butter. Once again, she stared at the numerous options. Who knew eggs came in various sizes? She lifted the cocoa can from the buggy and re-read the recipe. It simply listed eggs. The size must be optional. She grabbed a carton of large, doing the math to see how many batches she could make with a dozen.

After counting the items in her cart, she decided she'd best stop shopping since she had to be able to handle her bags on the bus.

With her merchandise paid for, she slung her purse and school bag onto her arms then gathered the two grocery sacks. She squealed faintly. *I'm the proud owner of my own groceries.* A young clerk opened the door for her as she made her way outside, shifting the bags for a better view in front of her.

"Ouch!" Marjorie grimaced at the pain. She had twisted her ankle on the curb. She tried to balance the bags as she righted herself, but one bag slipped from her arm. Of course, it was the bag with the eggs. She watched the goo of broken eggs ooze onto the sidewalk and atop her shoes. Dadgum. The eggs, which had been gingerly placed at the top of the bag, lay scattered on the pavement. "I'm an idiot. An injured idiot."

"Marjorie, let me help you." Relief mingled with embarrassment. Who had seen her trip and came to her rescue?

Tears rolled down her cheeks. Her ankle throbbed. Her pride hurt.

She turned to find Stewart next to her. The thought of his being here never occurred to her. He crouched. "Mind if I look at your ankle?" Marjorie nodded, appreciating the gesture. Pain wasn't selective of its rescuer. Stewart's fingers were gentle against her ankle as he patted the area. She sucked in a breath when he touched the left side.

"Sorry. I think you twisted it. It's not swelling or bruising, so I don't think its sprained or broken. Try putting pressure on it."

Marjorie let out a breath and flattened her foot. The ankle rebelled slightly, but she could stand on it. Stewart took her elbow and moved her toward a bench outside the store. She limped beside him.

"I'll get someone to clean this up and grab you some more eggs."

"Thank you." Those were the only words she could muster.

Within a moment, Wanda stood beside the bench. "Stewart said you tripped."

The woman sat beside her and took one of the grocery sacks. "We're going to drive you home. You can't ride the bus and walk on this ankle."

"Oh, that's kind, but I'll be all right."

"Nonsense."

. . .

Thank goodness Stewart drove. Images of her seated beside him in the back seat of Valene's car had flashed through her mind. Instead, Valene sat beside her. She glanced at her feet, propped up in the most lady-like manner possible, on her boss's legs. Wanda held a bag of groceries up front while the other rested on the floorboard beside Marjorie's belongings. The evening sky lacked luster, other than the full moon that seemed to boast in its dominance. She wished she were in the convertible with Daniel, the top down and the night breeze blowing her hair as she looked up into the sky. The evening news played on the radio.

Her three escorts chatted boisterously, and Marjorie wondered why they turned on the radio. She enjoyed the trio's camaraderie and found herself mixing in the conversation.

"It's the next house on the right."

Stewart shifted the car into a lower gear.

Theo lay on the lawn looking up at the sky. The boy made a habit of watching for planes flying overhead. Daniel had told her that the house stood beneath one of the flight paths.

With much ado, the trio assisted her out of the car and settled the grocery bags with Stewart. Theo came running.

"Miss Marjorie, who's this?"

"This is Stewart from work. He and some friends from work drove me home after I twisted my ankle."

"Mo-ommmmmmm. Marjorie is hurt." The next street over likely heard of her demise. Marjorie imagined porch lights flicking on down the row of houses.

With a hint of gallantry, Theo put his arm through Marjorie's as best he could with the difference in their heights. "Let me help you."

The screen door slammed as Lucy and Tali trotted toward her.

A dust storm of commotion swirled around as her condition was diagnosed.

"Who is he?" Tali cast Stewart an unwelcome look.

Marjorie introduced him and relayed the story of her accident. From the car, Valene and Wanda offered a wave from where they had settled back in their seats.

"Let's get her inside, so she can ice it." Stewart turned toward the front door.

Tali took off in a blur.

Mrs. Buckler slipped her arm around Marjorie's waist, and Theo followed suit. Stewart moved ahead and to open the screen door as he balanced the bags when Leland Buckler appeared. Introductions were quick and Mr. Buckler took the bags. Marjorie looked over her shoulder while being escorted to the couch.

"Thank you, Stewart. I would have been in a mess without your help. A batch of brownies is coming your way."

"Do you need a ride to beauty school tomorrow?"

She'd not thought about that dilemma, but chivalrous or not, he wasn't going to be the solution.

"I'll work something out, but thank you."

Stewart nodded and bid his goodbyes, then left. The oddity of his role tonight conflicted with her distaste of him. Perhaps she'd seen him at his best. Perhaps she had misjudged him somewhat.

"I'm taking you to school. I'll drop off Leland and then you." Mrs. Buckler's arm tightened around Marjorie's waist. "I suspect Daniel will want to pick you up." She smiled, and Marjorie felt her face blush.

No sooner had Theo and his mom settled her on the couch than Tali wiggled the phone receiver at her. "It's for you."

Marjorie tilted her head to one side and wrinkled her brows. Tali grinned and stretched the phone cord toward her.

"Hello?"

The voice on the other end voiced his concern.

"Daniel. I'm fine. Just a twisted ankle, I think." His concern made her heart dance.

News sprinted in the Buckler home for Daniel to already know about her mishap. Marjorie smiled at Tali, who hovered. Daniel's words confirmed her suspicion. His sister had phoned him and offered a brief explanation, "Marjorie is bad hurt," when he answered.

No doubt that Tali was staking Daniel's claim as her knight in shining armor in opposition to seeing Stewart helping her tonight.

Marjorie retold her story, answering every question her friend-boyfriend asked. "Tali propped my leg on a pillow, Theo brought me cola, and your mom just placed an ice pack on my foot. And if I am hearing things correctly, I think your dad is putting up my groceries. I hear cabinets opening and shutting."

Mrs. Buckler shooed her kids away, giving Marjorie some privacy. She breathed a sigh of relief. Now she could talk freely.

"Stay put. There's nothing you can do here." She laughed. "No, sir, you're not rejected."

When Daniel brought up the dilemma of walking to the bus stop, Marjorie explained. "Your mom is driving your dad to work, then me to school."

"Yes, you're picking me up in the afternoon. That's just what your mom predicted you'd say. Hey, I was going to call you tonight anyway." His tease at the honor of a girl-calling-a-boy made her laugh. "I have good news."

She shared the conversation she'd had with the school administrator. Daniel's response seemed a mixture of relief and excitement.

"You had such a good idea, so I doubt you'll ever be released from the dance committee." How she'd enjoy seeing his eyes light up with her teasing.

Daniel's voice became a bit husky when he shared that he had a question for her. She shifted and her ankle twinged, but the pain seemed to dissipate as he asked her to join him on a genuine date.

"Fancy yourself up. I'll be wearing my best suit and tie. Be hungry. And don't you worry about that foot for our date. I'll take care of you."

Both the ice on her foot and her heart were liquefying.

12

While Tali had mocked a swoon at the news of her official date with Daniel, Mrs. Buckler had scooped up a piece of paper and made a list. Dress, jewelry, shoes, evening bag. Marjorie had hair and nails covered.

"We'll go through things and find the rest. Thanks to law firm dinners, I've got lots of choices for you," Mrs. Buckler had assured her as she sat on the edge of Marjorie's bed the night before. Since the kind woman exceeded her by two inches in height and one two more in width, the words seemed more a suggestion than a solution. "And since we are sharing clothes, call me 'Lucy.'"

. . .

An array of students bent over shampoo bowls practiced shampooing on each other. Marjorie shifted the position of her good foot as she leaned over the bowl, careful not to disrupt her other leg propped at the knee on a chair. Hobbling in one high heel and a bandage on a date could prove to be challenging.

"Careful."

"Oops." Marjorie glanced at her fellow student, Evelyn, the subject of the shampoo exercise. She'd managed to spray the poor girl's face with water. My word, even though she had a good track record at work, what if she did something like that to a customer, such as Wanda Darden? She cringed. Marjorie yanked a towel from the overhead shelf and began to dab Evelyn's cheeks. "I'm so sorry."

"Foot hurting?"

"Mind wandering."

Evelyn giggled. "Tell me. I'm a captive audience."

Marjorie glanced around the large teaching salon. A hustle and bustle stirred the air as her class practiced their skills on one another. Some pairs chatted, while others worked in silence. The morning lecture came to mind. *An attentive beautician can surmise whether a customer wants to chat or not.* Apparently, Evelyn hoped for some scoop, so Marjorie obliged.

"Daniel is taking me on a date. I'm supposed to dress fancy. And be hungry." As the words danced from her mind and into the open air, Marjorie imagined herself as a princess at last. Her prince had not brought her a glass slipper; rather he'd awakened her from a deep sleep and brought her to life. Granted, his kiss was still missing, but she hoped in time it would come.

Every good and perfect gift. The passage from her Bible reading last night filled her with gratitude. Yes, Daniel was a gift in her life. And God was not an uncaring entity, mindless of her plight. *Every day I realize more how near you've always been.* The orphan had neither been fatherless nor neglected. She'd simply ignored the heavenly Father's biddings and offerings while He lingered patiently nearby. Her new daily habit of reading the Bible and praying opened her eyes to the relational God.

She and Evelyn halted their conversation while the instructor stood and watched Marjorie's scrubbing techniques and final rinse.

Marjorie patted Evelyn's hair with a towel, then wrapped it with another before hopping to the styling chair.

She situated her injured ankle on a foot stool, then combed and sectioned Evelyn's hair before calling the instructor to judge her work. "Excellent." Fulfillment swirled inside her at the teacher's opinion.

Evelyn boasted thick hair with a slight, springy curl. "Your hair is perfect for pin curls." Marjorie lifted a section of damp hair with a comb, placed the tip of her index finger at the end of the strand, and wound the hair around it. Sliding her finger off the wound hair, she clipped the curl with a hair pin. Once she examined her first curl, she got to work on the rest of Evelyn's hair. The conversation over the date ceased as she focused on her work.

"All done." Marjorie examined her work, gently eyeing and patting each section of hair.

Evelyn nodded her head to see if the curls stayed in place. "Feels tight and secure. Now, back to what we were talking about before. Do you have a fancy dress? Because if not, I think we're about the same size. I have two dresses that I think will be perfect for your date. One is black. The other is red. I'll bring them here tomorrow."

Marjorie squealed, then grimaced when several students glanced her way. Evelyn chuckled. Would Daniel prefer her in elegant black or hot rod red like his convertible? "Evelyn, you're my fairy godmother."

"In that case, I must bring you glass slippers too."

"One will do."

They both laughed.

"Marjorie Mullins, after I've dressed and jeweled you, mister history teacher will be so stunned, he won't be able to recall who discovered America."

"Let's hope he won't care who did at that moment."

With Evelyn settled under the dryer, Marjorie hopped to the towel bin and deposited the used towels, then returned to their shampoo station to clean up.

I must look a sight, hopping around on one foot. Her ankle brushed the side of the shampoo chair and she winced.

Who am I kidding? Hobbling like this Friday night, I'll feel more like the village idiot than a princess.

She hobbled back to the styling station.

"Rest that foot while you wait on Evelyn's hair to dry." The instructor turned the styling chair toward Marjorie, and she obliged by lowering it and plopping her bottom onto the seat. Her stomach growled, but noon was an hour away.

The bell on the front door jingled, and Marjorie glanced over the half wall topped with glass petitions which separated the small reception and waiting area from the training salon. A male figure exited.

She hadn't heard him enter. Other than deliveries, few men entered the beauty school. She leaned forward and squinted, trying to see the man who was now in the parking lot. Something looked familiar about him.

Oh, no. What was Stewart doing here? Would he never stop appearing out of nowhere?

The receptionist stood, grabbed something, then headed toward her.

Crutches.

Marjorie jerked her head down and stared at her perfectly manicured fingers, picking at an imaginary hangnail. Maybe, maybe, maybe those crutches weren't for her. Another gift from Stewart.

But she had to admit she needed them.

"Marjorie?"

Yep, the crutches were for her. Of course.

"A gentleman just left these for you."

The injured student looked up from nursing her ankle.

"Thanks." Marjorie noticed a piece of paper taped to one of the crutches.

"Now you won't have to hobble." The receptionist smiled and leaned the crutches against the styling chair before walking away.

Relief set in. She was worn with hobbling. Stewart had come to her rescue again.

Marjorie pulled the note from the crutch to read it.

I borrowed these from Hillhurst. I tried to adjust them to your size. Feel better soon. Stewart.

Marjorie raised one of the crutches in the air. "Cool! Now I gotta figure out how to use them."

Offers of assistance came her way, and within minutes Marjorie limped on crutches toward the dryer where Evelyn sat. She raised the bonnet and felt for any remaining moisture around the curls.

"Whoa!" Marjorie hobbled, but Evelyn's hand steadied her just before she lost total balance.

"Thanks. I gotta get used to these things."

"Was that Daniel who brought the crutches?"

"Oh, heavens, no."

"Do you know who it was?"

"Yes."

"Who?"

"Stewart."

"Your rescuer."

"Stop it. Can we just get you seated and let me finish my assignment?"

Between the pain in her ankle, the effort to walk on crutches, and the angst of Evelyn tagging Stewart as Daniel, Marjorie wanted to change the subject.

Evelyn grinned. "Touchy."

Marjorie regretted her snippy comments and offered her friend an apology as she rested the crutches on the cabinet and propped her leg back up.

"Well, he's cute. I'd like to meet him."

She bit her tongue at the comment and glanced at Evelyn's reflection in the mirror. Her classmate was cute—sparkling eyes, light freckles, high cheekbones. Her red hair and big smile were to die for. Confidence showed in her face. Why would she want to meet Stewart? The beautician-in-training checked her response.

"Are you serious?"

"Why not? I know he gets on your nerves, but the guy's gone out of his way to help you. He seems nice. I think he's kinda cute."

Maybe she should move Stewart to the "nice guy" category.

"Well, maybe you could come by the Wright Do some time, and I'll introduce you. He works at the nursing home."

"Girl, you got a deal. Hey, did I tell you my cousin moved out, and I'm looking for a roommate?"

Stewart? No way.

"Close that mouth of yours, Marjorie. I know what you're thinking. I'm looking for a girl roommate."

"Whew." Marjorie began to unwind Evelyn's pin curls.

"Does Stewart have a sister?"

"Yes. My boss."

"Oh, right. Does she need a place to live?"

"She's older and has a place of her own."

"Didn't hurt to ask."

Marjorie laughed.

. . .

"I hardly recognize myself. Great job." Marjorie leaned forward in her salon chair and turned her head back and forth admiring what she saw in the salon mirror. She rarely wore her hair teased, but the extra fullness seemed a pleasant change. Her flipped ends blended nicely with the extra height. Evelyn's reflection beamed from behind the style chair. "Thank you. It's easy to make you look good though."

Was it? She'd never been sure. Daniel seemed to think she was pretty.

Though weary from exerting energy to hop, hobble, and crutch, Marjorie felt good at the day's end. Both she and Evelyn had gotten good marks on the shampoo, set, and style exercise on one another.

The atmosphere in the training salon mimicked her own mood. Conversations were few as students cleaned up the stations. She supposed most students felt as hungry and ready for home as she did.

The bell on the front door jingled, and with a dreaded sense of déjà vu, Marjorie turned her head toward the reception area. *Please don't let it be Stewart here to check on me.*

Daniel, his tie loose and shirt sleeves rolled to his elbows, approached her with a gorgeous grin and…

Crutches.

Her insides shifted. So eager was Marjorie to be near him, she forgot and tried to stand on her twisted ankle. *Ouch.* Lifting it back off the floor, she saw her crutches propped against the counter.

"Daniel."

He stood next to her chair. "Hi. Am I interrupting?"

"No. We're done."

He did a double-take when he saw her hair.

She introduced Daniel to Evelyn, then saw him eyeing her crutches.

"I borrowed these from the basketball coach, but I see you've got some."

"They came from Hillhurst."

He chuckled and set down the pair he held. "They rode the bus here on their own?"

Evelyn laughed.

"No, Stewart brought them around lunch." The words dried her tongue on their way out.

"That's good. You had them for this afternoon." He offered her a hand and used the other to grab the Hillhurst crutches.

Why did he choose that pair?

He braced her from behind as she situated herself. Warm breath grazed her ear. "Are you steady?"

"Yes."

He released her.

Her eyes connected with Evelyn, who still stood behind the style chair.

Daniel came around her and grabbed the crutches he'd brought. "You ready?"

Evelyn spoke up. "Let me get her bag."

With her friend gone, Marjorie looked Daniel in the eyes. "Thank you for getting those."

"Anything for you, ma'am."

"Should I leave a pair here—you know, one for work and one for home?" *Great idea, if I say so myself.*

"Well, you'd have to get here or anywhere else on crutches, so no need to have two pair at the school."

Duh.

Evelyn returned with a bag in one hand and a purse in the other. Daniel took them, and the three of them bid goodbye.

"Ready?" Daniel motioned toward the door.

They fumbled here and there getting her and the crutches situated in the car. Daniel slid into his seat then leaned toward her.

"You okay?"

"Whew. Yes. Hobbling is hard work."

"Let's get you home. But can I ask you a question?"

"Sure."

"Are you gonna have a new hair style?"

Marjorie laughed. "No. Evelyn styled it for an assignment. What do you think?"

"Looks like she did a good job."

"So, you like it?"

He clicked his tongue a couple of times. "You look pretty no matter what. But the way you do your own hair knocks my socks off."

She wouldn't be teasing her hair Friday night.

"Well, thank you, Daniel Buckler."

The draw between them felt intense.

Marjorie took in a quick breath. Something was different. Something shifted in her when Daniel had walked into the training salon. The brevity of their acquaintance no longer mattered. Friendship alone would no longer satisfy.

He leaned forward in his seat and pulled a thin, blue box from beneath it.

"I have something else for you."

"Ooooh, how sweet." She took the box.

"And if Stewart already gave you one, I'll have to be more on my toes."

Her smiled fell away but she yanked it back in place.

• • •

His teeth split the pencil into three parts. He spit bits of lead and wood onto the grass, then snatched up the slobbery pieces from his lap and tossed them into the pond. *What a jerk.* The water peeking through the cat tails looked black and deep beneath the cloudy night sky. As though a person could get pulled beneath and never return. The croak of the bullfrogs seemed a warning to keep away.

He scrubbed his hands over his face then ran them through his hair before leaning back onto his elbows. Normally, the pond behind his neighborhood offered him a chance to clear his mind, but not tonight. Its eerie setting matched his self-loathing hard at work.

Daniel could not erase the image of Marjorie's face morphing from excited to puzzled over his stupid Stewart remark. He'd ruined the moment between them and likely tainted any pleasure she might have while wearing the watch he'd given her. He'd never struggled with jealousy on this level before, not even when Conrad married Candace.

He nodded his head though no one was there to see it. That truth should tell him something about his relationship with Candace. He'd been angry over someone taking what belonged to him, over his life being disrupted. But he hadn't been jealous over someone else's affection for his bride-to-be.

He wasn't embarrassed that Marjorie already had a pair of crutches. He was disappointed that another man had thought about her needs and went out of his way to meet them before he could. Stewart had done a thoughtful thing.

Now he understood Marjorie's concerns over how he might feel about Candace. He blew out a breath. He was fretting over a man that had an elementary school crush. Marjorie had to worry about a former a bride-to-be.

Sure, she'd smiled and made a big deal over the watch he gave her. Promising to wear it on the date like he'd hoped. Rather than apologizing over his ill-worded joke, and recovering the tenderness between them, he turned their time into a meeting to discuss details between the dance committee and the beauty school. He'd not dallied a moment at his family home, leaving under the pretense that he had a lot of work to do. The pretense was weak at its best and a lie at its worst. Marjorie hadn't protested his departure, but her pursed lips told him she'd seen through his excuse.

I messed up.

Sitting here pouting was no solution. He should get up, go telephone Marjorie, and apologize.

He grabbed the jacket he'd tossed over a rock and trotted back home. His and Marjorie's world needed to be made right again. Not bothering to lock the door behind him in case Candace showed up, he dropped his jacket on the floor, then dialed the Buckler home.

Life is filled with pleasure, but Daniel reckoned that few surpassed the camaraderie between a man and woman in each other's romantic favor. He hung up the phone after they bid good-night. Their world moved back on its axis. He couldn't wait to drive her to beauty school tomorrow.

He locked the door, hung up his jacket, then opened a cola. He really did have some papers to grade.

The telephone startled him.

He grinned. Did Marjorie miss him already?

He lifted the receiver. "Hello."

"Danny."

Cola seeped back up his throat.

"Don't telephone me, Candace."

"I'm pregnant."

13

Daniel stared into his coffee cup as his dad sat across his table from him. The clock struck 10:00 PM.

"Do Mom or Marjorie know you're here?"

"Your mom does. She knew it was you on the phone. Marjorie was in her room."

"Thanks for coming over." He let out a heavy breath. "How could Conrad abandon his pregnant wife?"

"They married in such haste. I'd guess life inside the bedroom was all he wanted. But Son, my stars, I can't figure why this has you pacing the floor."

"I almost married her."

His Dad cleared his throat. "The only reason that fact would matter is if you still have feelings for her."

Daniel had no romantic feelings for Candace. Indeed, it was Marjorie who saturated him.

"I'm in love with Marjorie."

"You're talking in circles."

Daniel stalled. Leland Buckler had a knack for waiting on a person to speak rather than filling the silence. Daniel admired the trait, but not tonight.

"I have no romantic feelings for Candace. I almost loathe her. But I introduced her and Conrad. Who knew he was such a jerk? Dad, I keep thinking that I planned on being her husband."

"Do not tell me you plan to marry that woman now?"

"What? No! But I do feel some warped sense of responsibility."

"It's not your baby." The twist of his father's head turned the statement into a question. Daniel felt insulted.

"No, Dad. How could you even wonder?"

"Because that warped sense of responsibility you feel confuses me."

"Maybe it's a moral dilemma instead of a feeling of responsibility."

"So, her honor is your moral dilemma? You'd marry the girl who walked out on you, whom you admitted you don't love, to protect her reputation?"

"No. She plans to abort it." He watched his father's face grow stern. "Dad, that's wrong and risky, but she's determined. She found a doctor just below the Oklahoma border."

Daniel sensed the lawyer at work in his father.

"Explain what that has to do with you. That's not your moral dilemma."

"I tried to talk her into keeping the baby. Suggested she could give it up for adoption."

The irony of that thought twisted his brain and formed a headache. "And she asked me to drive her to the clinic, but I said no. Should I go, and on the way try to talk her out of aborting it? That's my moral dilemma."

"That's absurd, Son. If you can't talk her out of it here, you're not going to talk her out of it on the way there. And it's not your place to talk her out of anything."

The air felt heavy with his dad's presence. Leland Buckler sat before him, more the father a little boy than the confidante of a young man.

"If she keeps it, she'd likely struggle as a single mom."

"And if you play any part in persuading her one way or the other, she could claim you're the negligent father—or she could play on your sympathy and keep seeking your help."

His spirit knotted, acknowledging the difference between right and ridiculous.

His father stood from his seat. "I doubt you've prayed over this."

He hadn't. He'd reacted and called his dad for advice on his thoughts.

His father, acting more like Leland Buckler, attorney-at law, than Dad, stood and opened the side door off the kitchen. "I argue that there is only one reasonable thing you should do. You're smart enough to figure it out. I pray to God that you do." The door closed behind him, leaving Daniel a bit shamed. His father's coffee sat there untouched and cold, a testament to the distaste his reasoning caused them both.

Daniel tossed the unused coffee into the sink. Not bothering to wash the cups, he slapped the kitchen light off and shuffled toward his couch. He plopped himself down and hung his head between his knees. Never had his house felt so confining; even the walls seemed to be in judgment of him. Maybe he'd head back to the pond.

Grabbing a blanket and flashlight from the hall closet, he headed outside, quickly returning to grab his keys and lock his door.

The air stung his cheeks. Good, maybe it would stir his senses. He must resemble a lunatic roaming the street this late. The night that should have been the eve of his wedding hadn't knotted his gut like this one. There had been no decision to make that night—no moral dilemma. Candace had broken their engagement, and he'd not put up a fight.

Not put up a fight? He settled onto the blanket while the question taunted him. Did his soul know then what his mind didn't? Who wouldn't fight for the woman he was about to marry? Maybe deep humiliation stopped him from chasing Candace that night she walked out of the church sanctuary. Now he wondered if horrifying relief had stopped him in his tracks.

Yet, here he sat a couple years later agonizing over that same woman, with no romantic connection as an excuse. Aborting a baby was a desperate decision. Could he just ignore it? Conrad and Candace had done him wrong, and he sure didn't want them doing an innocent baby wrong.

His confusion baffled him.

"God, I'm a wreck. What do I do?"

Marjorie's lovely face came to mind. He closed his eyes and drank in the joy of her. He sensed her touch and nestled in the imagined nearness of her. His love for her filled him, overflowing to saturate his skin. He stilled his thoughts on the image of her eyes. Marjorie, a life unopened, alone until their paths collided. The little girl in her still struggled with feeling unwanted, while the woman in her seemed on the verge of casting enduring trust on him. Would any moral dilemma justify breaking that bond?

"God, tell me what I'm not seeing about myself."

He never thought he wanted revenge on Candace, yet here in the still night, he realized that he may have. Somewhere in the crevices of his human nature, perhaps he'd sought ill will on her since the abandonment. Did her being pregnant and abandoned actually satisfy him?

Maybe his motive to save the baby wasn't moral at all. Perhaps it was overcompensation for some misguided justice.

He looked to the black heavens and knew to stay put. God had more to teach him.

At last, he pushed himself up, steadying his sleeping legs, and trekked back home. Setting an alarm, he plopped himself into bed for what little sleep might come his way.

When the alarm clock rang, Daniel pressed the button to turn it off, then rolled onto his side. Four in the morning had afforded him three hours of sleep, not near enough, but he had a stack of papers to grade. He rubbed his face with his hands then threw back the covers. Sitting up, he recalled the late night and early morning hours. His conclusion had not changed from when he left the pond.

His Dad had challenged him to examine his motive and pray. He had.

And now he knew what he needed to do—that one reasonable thing his dad alluded to.

• • •

"Operator, can you dial the number for Conrad Petty in Mikel, Louisiana?" As the operator connected the line, Daniel's stomach knotted. His roommate had always been an early riser in college, and he was banking on that habit now.

The phone rang. Daniel paced. When Conrad answered, all thoughts he'd had of talking Candace out of the abortion felt absurd. That duty belonged to the man on the other end of the telephone line. Why hadn't he realized that immediately last night?

He swallowed. "Conrad, its Daniel. I know it's early, but can we talk?"

14

Marjorie poured more syrup on her breakfast. "The pancakes at the orphanage must have been rubber. Who knew they should be light and fluffy?" She tossed a wide smile at Lucy. "Will you teach me your recipe?"

"Of course." Lucy's own smile wilted. Marjorie studied Mr. Buckler, who sat pensive. Maybe perturbed. Theo resembled his normal sleepy and hungry self. Were it not for the chatter of Tali, who proved to be both a night and morning person, the Buckler family had little to say this morning. The air felt dense. Perhaps there had been a disagreement between Mr. and Mrs. Buckler. She suddenly felt like an intruder and finished her pancakes in a hurry before hopping to the sink to wash her dishes.

Glancing at her watch, she realized she had ten minutes until time to leave. She situated herself on the crutches.

"Marjorie, we'll do that cooking lesson soon." Lucy's tone resonated with doubt.

"I look forward to it." She shrugged internally at the brief exchange, then hobbled toward the bathroom to brush her teeth.

After their make-up telephone call last night, Marjorie's mind had dwelt on nothing but Daniel. She rinsed her toothbrush, then gargled, flashing a genuine smile in the mirror. Though she knew there was no reason for Daniel to feel jealous over Stewart, his admittance of being disappointed he hadn't helped her fast enough was sweet.

"Now I realize how you might feel about Candace," he'd said. Somehow that confession smothered the very feelings it had acknowledged. His relating to her doubts, made them disappear.

She examined her heart. Moving forward, not only professionally, but personally, had her bouncing on her toes—on her good foot. With the help of God and support of Daniel, maybe the day after their date, she'd face the past explained in her envelope then cling to the future awaiting her. If the news upset her, she didn't want to ruin their time together on Friday.

The oddity of the morning continued when Marjorie arrived in the living room, and it was void of Lucy and Mr. Buckler. Unlike yesterday, no one waited to assist her to the car. Whatever had happened with the Bucklers in the hours between sleep and wake put the household off kilter. The clock near the television read 8:15 AM. Time to leave. She opened the coat closet and attempted to yank her jacket loose.

"Be careful. I'll get it."

She welcomed Tali's voice and shifted to see the girl. "Thanks. Wanna help me make brownies tonight?

"If Daniel will let me. He might want you to himself. You know, be the big protector and everything." She flexed her muscles.

"You mean, he might get under foot?"

Tali nodded her agreement. "We can make him clean up."

"I like your thinking, Tali."

The Bucklers entered hand-in-hand. Lucy's face appeared blotchy, and in an instant, the room seemed to tilt. Without a doubt, something had gone amiss. Marjorie glanced at Tali, who simply lifted her shoulders.

"Ready for us to get you in the car?" Marjorie felt Lucy's gentle pat on her arm.

"Yes ma'am." Not only was she ready to get in the car, Marjorie felt ready to be away from the tension. She was no expert on the Buckler family after only days of acquaintance, but she'd yet to see a hint of this gloom from any of them.

With the limited dignity her injury allowed, Marjorie braced herself between Mr. And Mrs. Buckler and hopped down the front steps. Tali followed, then handed her the crutches.

"With you two beside me, let me see how much pressure I can put on my foot." She lowered her injured and well-manicured appendage to the grass and applied pressure. "Ouch." Oh well, she'd be sporting crutches on her date.

"Whew." Marjorie plopped her bottom onto the backseat and blew out a breath. She caught a glimpse of the sky. No gloominess there. The autumn sun blended its warmth with the crisp air and touched her cheek.

"All set?" Lucy had her hand on the door handle as she spoke.

"Yes." Marjorie waved to Tali, then flattened the wrinkles in her uniform.

Before Lucy had shut the door, a police car sped down the residential street, sending leaves into an upward spiral and into the yard. Marjorie startled as the siren blared.

"Oh, goodness." Lucy abandoned shutting the door and moved in the direction the police care had gone.

Emerging from the front passenger seat, Mr. Buckler took his place near his wife. Marjorie leaned out the car to see the police pull into a driveway.

Tali ran toward her mother. "Why is a police car at Rusty's house?"

Marjorie's curiosity heightened at the mention of the student who'd plowed into her, thankfully, and who seemed to hold a special place in Daniel's heart.

The four of them remained silent as two policemen made their way to Rusty's front porch. Leland broke the silence. "Well, Lucy, maybe you can check on them when you return."

"If you think that's best, Leland."

"Only if the police car is gone."

A subtle wave moved over the street as neighbors eased into yards, hovered on porches, or leaned out doorways.

"Tali, I see the bus coming. Get your satchel and your brother."

"Theo, the bus is here," Tali shouted as she took off toward the house.

Marjorie and the Bucklers settled themselves into the car. "Wait." Marjorie pointed. "I see people coming out of Rusty's house."

Lucy turned off the ignition and Mr. Buckler got out of the car. As the police car exited the driveway, its siren breaking the quiet, a couple in a white sedan followed. To Marjorie's surprise, the driver of the car slowed long enough to roll down his window and shout to the Bucklers.

"Rusty got hurt on the way to school and is in the hospital."

Lucy's hand flew to her mouth. "Dear Lord, help him."

Tali and Theo waved their arms seeking attention. "What happened?" Tali's question rang in the air.

"Later," Lucy shouted. "Scoot."

Tali huffed, then the two darted toward the stop sign to wait on the bus.

The chaos concluded, and Mr. Buckler rejoined Marjorie and his wife in the car.

Whatever tension had thrown the morning off its axis now seemed replaced by concern.

. . .

Marjorie yawned. The morning felt tedious. It wasn't that she didn't want to learn about roller curls; indeed, the Pie Lady at The Wright Do seemed to have the perfect head shape for the style. The issue was her distracted mind. It moved in and out of focus on the lesson, and she hoped she hadn't missed anything important. Her thoughts kept meandering to Rusty, and every time they did, she said a prayer. She wondered if Daniel and other teachers had been told what happened.

But they weren't the only things adding to her distracted state. She was crawling out of her skin with excitement to try on the attire Evelyn had brought with her today. Then she couldn't stop her mind from wondering how the Dance Do event would turn out. Not to be ignored, the unopened envelope taunted her with anticipation one moment and anxiety another.

How full her life had become in the last month. Sometimes she could scarcely take it in without losing her breath. Loneliness had been her lifetime shadow, though she'd never sensed its presence until it vanished—pushed away by new responsibilities, a family of sorts, and God. The Heavenly Father would have vanquished the shadow long ago had she not closed Him out.

She cast a look toward Evelyn seated next to her, and the two of them shared a grin. Marjorie wasn't sure who felt more excited about dolling her up. Even though she knew little of Evelyn beyond her life here at the school, she enjoyed her company. At last, lunch break arrived.

Marjorie grabbed Evelyn by the arm. "I can't wait to see what you brought." The two of them slipped out to Evelyn's car.

"Sorry I can't help you lug this in."

Evelyn tucked a shoe box under each arm, grabbed a garment bag, then slid her fingers through the plastic handle of a pink cosmetic case. She pushed the car door closed with her hip.

"Let's go, princess"

Marjorie giggled the entire trip to the ladies' room, warmed by the gathering of girls who followed her and Evelyn. She was not the only one eager to see her transformation.

"Let's start with the black." Evelyn unzipped the garment bag.

"Oh! It's gorgeous." Marjorie covered her mouth and squealed, then sunk into the magic of the moment, well, as magic as it could be with crutches tucked beneath her arms.

While Evelyn and the others waited, Marjorie situated herself and changed into the black dress.

"Here I come." The black chiffon rested against her body in a perfect fit. She had never dressed in anything so fine. Despite the oohs and aahs in the room, an image in her mind held her captive, while the image in the mirror did the same. A little orphan girl, clad in a drab uniform, looked up at her, eyes twinkling with wonder. Her five-year-old self whispered, "You look beautiful. I want to be you one day."

I'm my own wish come true.

"Well, what do you think?" Evelyn's voice broke her trance.

"I can't believe that's me. It fits perfect."

"It's divine, but let's try on the red."

If the little orphan in her had appeared to see the red dress, she'd have spun in delight. The room buzzed with approval. Though the black dress looked beautiful, the red dress caused her eyes and hair to pop, as though they hadn't existed before this moment. The dress clung and flared in just the right places, accentuating the best of her figure.

"This is it." She whispered to the little girl inside her.

Evelyn bounced on her toes. "Marjorie, you're a dream."

She had to agree as tears of the best sort misted her eyes and made them sparkle.

A shoe for her right foot was next.

With the lunch hour nearing its end, Marjorie's attire for Friday evening was selected. The jewelry Evelyn brought complemented the watch Daniel had given her.

"I don't have a silver or red clutch. You'll have to use the black."

"That's okay. Mrs. Buckler has silver. And she's eager to help me."

As if the woman hadn't helped her already with the rigmarole of getting a bath. They'd worked out a system that spared them both embarrassment—like a mother would do for a daughter. Marjorie would be thrilled to use the woman's clutch.

Five hours later, Marjorie headed from the classroom toward the exit, excited to see Daniel. Evelyn followed behind with everything she would need for her special date.

She pushed open the front door to discover Lucy waiting in her car. No red convertible and no Daniel in sight.

As the two of them approached, Lucy rolled down the window.

"I'm here to take you home. Daniel called from the hospital. He went to visit Rusty and is still there."

"Oh. Of course. Do you know what happened?" Marjorie glanced at Evelyn. "Rusty is the neighbor I told you about." Evelyn nodded.

"Seems Rusty was standing in the back of the bus as it was rolling to a stop at a traffic light. That boy Curtis we saw at Ludy's stood up and shoved him into the bus's back emergency door while the bus was still moving. The door latch was faulty, and Rusty fell onto the street."

Marjorie gasped. "Is he going to be okay?"

"Yes, but he has some broken bones. And is quite scraped up."

"Poor Rusty. I wonder why Curtis did that."

"I wonder why Rusty was standing in the aisle," Lucy added.

"That's awful," Evelyn interjected.

"Oh, Mrs. Buckler, this is my friend, Evelyn."

The two acknowledged each other.

"Between the two of you dressing me, I just might be a knock out tomorrow night, if I say so myself."

Lucy's smile resurrected the oddity of that morning, but then transformed into a full grin.

Marjorie hoped the Bucklers would straighten out what had gone crooked.

"There's no doubt Daniel will be speechless when he sees her tomorrow night. I was today." Evelyn hugged Marjorie, then said her goodbyes.

· · ·

Theo handed Marjorie the dice with a mock snarl on his face. "You are not going to beat me again tonight, Yahtzee Queen."

186

Marjorie laughed. "I dare you to beat me."

His mouth spread in a grin. "Is that a double-dog dare?

"You know it is."

"Theo, you're so dramatic. Marjorie beats you at this game because she is S.M.A.R.T and you're N.O.T."

"Be nice to your brother." The command came from Mr. Buckler's lips, sounding worn and overused.

"I know how to spell, Tali. Especially three-letter-words. Ignore her, Marjorie. The dare is on."

Marjorie reached over the kitchen table and shook Theo's hand. "May the best man win."

"Woman," Tali inserted.

"You heard your father."

Marjorie covered her mouth to hide her grin. Lucy's retort sounded as weary as her husband's had.

"Lucy, you're first." Mr. Buckler got the game started.

Despite a hearty meal and a game together, something still felt off kilter between Daniel's parents. Looks between them seemed serious, as though the meatloaf and the dice game were a front.

The telephone rang, and Tali sprang into action.

"Hello."

She shook the phone at Marjorie and mouthed "Daniel"

"Is Rusty still alive?"

"Tali!" Her parents responded in unison. She shrugged at them, just as Marjorie hobbled the few steps and reached for the phone.

"Here's Marjorie."

She took the phone before propping against the counter.

"Hello."

His hello in return, though sounding tired, comforted her.

They talked about Rusty, then Daniel turned a bit mushy. She'd missed him, too, but she couldn't declare that in the presence of his family.

"Me, too. About you, I mean."

He laughed, assured her he couldn't wait to see her tomorrow night, then asked to speak to his father.

"Mr. Buckler, it's for you."

He scooted his chair back and took the phone from her.

"Hello, Son."

Marjorie wasn't trying to be nosey, but she couldn't help notice that Mr. Buckler stilled. The conversation became one-sided as he nodded up and down without offering a word in return.

At last, he directed a smile to his wife. "That's good news, Son."

Lucy's eyes widened, and she smiled back at her husband.

Marjorie had no idea what Daniel had shared with his dad, but all at once, the house righted itself, and life no longer felt off-kilter.

15

Daniel pulled the small piece of tissue from his chin and examined the shaving nick. Good, the dramatic bleed from the minuscule cut had stopped. He didn't consider himself a vain man, but he didn't want to be sporting tissue when he picked up Marjorie. A quick glance at his collar assured him it had been spared the drama.

He jiggled his tie knot, then smoothed the ruby red silk material with his hand. With a sigh, he stilled himself and examined the reflection in the mirror. His eyes stared beyond the physical person and into the soul of the man.

Nothing about him deserved another chance at romance. For that matter, nothing about him deserved the goodness of God. In the last twenty-four hours, he'd experienced the grace of God's guidance and been spared potential heartache. Thank God, he'd come to his senses about Candace and her baby. The moral decision belonged to Conrad and Candace. He'd pray for protection of the baby and even restoration for the marriage of the friends who betrayed him. But now, his intentions stopped there.

He wanted no secrets between him and Marjorie, so he needed to tell her about his halted stupidity, but not during the special night he had planned for her.

He put on his suit jacket, then moved to the living room and grabbed the red roses from the coffee table. The florist had wrapped them beautifully. He glanced around his abode. When Marjorie injured her foot, he rearranged his plans for their date—the Dallas Symphony would have to wait for another time. He had then thought to bring her here, cook dinner—not that he was good at it—then cozy up and listen to records, well in view of the large kitchen window, of course. That scenario didn't seem special enough.

Daniel grinned. The arrangements had fallen into place far better than he could have imagined. He hoped the evening would show Marjorie just how special she was. He lay the roses on the passenger seat of his spick and span convertible, then headed out.

He couldn't recall ever knocking at his family home, but tonight Daniel wasn't the boy who'd grown up within its walls. He was a man in love here to escort a beautiful woman. He tapped on the wooden door and stepped back, keeping the roses steady in his hand. The uneven click of a one-heeled gait announced Marjorie's arrival on the other side. From the corner of his eye, Daniel caught Tali peeking through the curtains. If he couldn't control himself and planted a kiss on Marjorie, then Tali would just have to be a witness.

The door squeaked lightly as someone pulled it open, and Marjorie stood before him, balanced on her crutches.

The earth and sky gave way. Her eyes sparkled, and the lids closed and opened in a blink. Her lips formed a lovely curve, and fitted behind red satin, her other curves teased him.

No one else existed in the moment.

"You look gorgeous, Marjorie. Stunning" Her countenance brightened.

"You are quite stunning yourself, Daniel."

He leaned back and noticed the whole of her. A silver necklace and matching earrings adorned her, while a small silver purse hung from her arm. The arm upon which the watch he gave her rested. Beneath that, a delicate hand showed off her trademark manicure. And, not one hair on her head looked teased. Every single thing about her was beautiful—even the wounded foot, with bright red painted toes.

"These are for you." He tilted the bouquet toward her, and she sniffed them. "But I'll hold them for now."

"They're beautiful. Thank you."

"Are you ready?" She nodded.

He called for Tali. "Hold these crutches and flowers, please."

He scooped Marjorie into his arms. She wrapped her arms around his neck as they headed toward the car.

"I can't wait to spend time with you." The whispered words tickled her ears.

Marjorie's breath warmed his neck when she whispered back. "I've been so excited about tonight."

His eyes caught hers. He really should lean down and kiss her lips, but he'd wait for the right moment. Then of their own accord, his lips grazed her cheek. He felt her smile.

Tali no doubt stood with her mouth ajar.

He opened the door and carefully released her into the seat.

"Don't go anywhere." He winked then trotted back to the house.

"Tali, your mouth is hanging open." He rubbed his sister's head, then took the crutches and flowers from her. "Don't wait up, little sis."

Running back to the car and tossing the crutches in the backseat, he paused before handing Marjorie the roses.

"Will these wrinkle your dress?"

"I don't think so."

He leaned over her and lay the flowers in the back seat.

"Just in case. And, by the way, you smell wonderful."

As he leaned up, she pulled his shoulder back down toward her and nudged his neck with her nose. "Likewise."

Their eyes connected.

Now, all he had to do was get behind the wheel and keep his eyes on the road. The second task would be near impossible with the gorgeous Funeral Lady seated next to him.

• • •

Daniel adjusted the radio to K-LAS, the only station that played classical music.

"Sounds nice."

He offered his hand, and Marjorie laced their fingers.

"If the weather were warmer, I'd lower the top to see the stars."

"It's quite a view."

His eyes rested on her. "Yes, it is."

Daniel mentally recapped the details he'd set in motion for the evening and glanced at his watch. In less than an hour everything should be in place and awaiting their arrival. He'd been previously unacquainted with any romantic part of his nature. He came to know it when he had to accommodate the date for Marjorie's injury. Once he dwelt on how to ease her inconvenience with crutches, the plan revealed itself much like his paintings that emerged stroke by stroke.

He grinned. His junior high students who got a note from their latest crush couldn't feel more excited than he did this moment.

Conversation flowed between them, though Daniel felt her words as much as he heard them. Wrapped in a feminine drawl, her voice seeped into the part of him designed by the Creator to love a woman. She filled him to overflowing that he could offer her in return. They were a source for one another.

Did she feel it?

Marjorie pointed to the new motel being built at the freeway. "We're leaving town?"

"Yes."

"Where are we going?"

He squeezed her hand. "Wait and see."

And she did, taking in the sights as though she'd never traveled outside their town of Hazel. Daniel sucked in a breath. Perhaps she hadn't.

"Marjorie, what's the furthest place you've ever traveled to?"

"Wherever we are now."

He turned to see her—eyes off the road. She tilted her chin and lifted her eyes in return.

"Daniel, this is my first adventure."

Something akin to pity rose like bile in his throat. He'd not give in to it. Instead, he'd embrace the moment with her.

"Marjorie." He literally didn't know what else to say. She must have realized that, for she returned the question and filled the silence.

"What's the most faraway place you've been?"

Man, he didn't want to answer.

"The Grand Canyon."

"I want to hear all about it."

The telling of his family's adventure filled the next few miles until Daniel pointed out a sign on the side of the freeway.

"Dallas?" Marjorie gasped, then turned her body in the seat. Her ankle twisted, and she winced. "Are you taking me to Dallas?"

"Careful. And yes, welcome to Big D."

He left the freeway, then jigged and jagged through streets until the site of their adventure came into view. He parked the car in front of a white, one-story building with yellow accents and Mexican architecture. Big orange letters spelled "Consuela's" near the entrance's wooden doors. Light shone through only two of the eight windows across the long building's front.

"No one else is here, Daniel. Are you sure this place is open?"

"Don't you worry your pretty head. It's both closed and open."

She wrinkled her brows before surrendering to a grin.

"Wait here." Daniel took the crutches to the doorway, then returned to her. Grabbing the roses, he handed them to her. Without warning, he once again scooped her into his arms, the roses pressed against his chin as she held them. He released her when she could brace herself on the crutches.

Daniel held the roses again, then opened the door. Hints of garlic and onion greeted them. A man wearing a gray, charro suit stood on the inside. "Welcome to Consuela's, Miss Marjorie." His Mexican accent was evident in his vowels and tongue rolls.

The restaurant appeared ready to serve guests but was empty, other than their host. To the right, where light had come through the windows, sat a table for two, lit with candles.

"Your table, Senorita."

Daniel stood behind his own chair while the host seated Marjorie and propped the crutches against an empty table, then maneuvered the place settings to make room for the roses.

"Dinner will be served."

"Thank you, Jose."

From a small hallway, a man dressed in a dark, Mariachi suit emerged and began strumming a guitar.

When Jose moved away, Daniel cleared his throat. "We have the place to ourselves. I hope you don't mind."

Marjorie's mouth opened delicately. "I'm stunned. And thrilled. How?"

For a moment, Daniel relished in the mystery, then finally shared how the evening had come about. When he happened to mention to his fellow teacher, Mrs. Cortes, that he had to re-think his plans for this evening, she suggested her husband might have a solution.

"So, it turns out Mr. Cortes is the meat supplier for Jose and this restaurant. It doesn't open to the public until next week, but Jose agreed to host a private dinner for the two of us."

Of course, Daniel didn't mention that he'd forked out a hefty wad of dough for the privacy. And he'd do it again.

Her eyes glistened in the candlelight. "I'm on cloud nine."

"And I'm having a blast watching you on that cloud."

. . .

The Mexican coffee warmed his throat as it washed down the last bite of flan. The blended sweetness of both proved a bit much for his palette. Across the table, Marjorie sipped her warm brew, having left the last bites of the shared custard for him. The evening was coming to an end.

Daniel had been in love when he entered the restaurant. He'd leave having fallen even deeper into the emotion.

"We match." Marjorie indicated her dress and his tie.

He'd not noticed. Well, he'd not noticed their matching, but he'd certainly taken intense notice of the red dress highlighting her features.

"We do." His top lip lifted at the corner. "You know, I still plan to paint your portrait."

Marjorie nodded, then set her cup on the saucer and reached for his hands. He obliged and clasped her fingers, his thumbs rubbing her knuckles.

She licked her lips, and he had to shift his feet to release the resulting impact. "You've given me a night that I think most women only dream of." He felt his face flush. "This meal tasted delicious. But I want you to know, I fell in love with you over a tater tot."

He replayed her declaration. *I fell in love with you.*

"That first night we went to Rosie's Diner on our not-a-date-date when you were everyday Daniel, the man of my imagination finally had a name and a face."

As though a strong wind sucked the building empty, Daniel once again found himself seeing only her. Emotion pressed into him, and he fought to breathe in a steady pace. Gazing at her beauty and vulnerability and hearing her confession of love, Daniel couldn't believe the danger he'd almost put their relationship in. He'd dubbed the force as morality, yet looking at Marjorie now, he realized it was nothing close to morality. He'd almost given in to the vortex that was Candace.

"Daniel? I hope you don't mind what I just said." Marjorie's voice hinted at embarrassment. She'd borne her soul, and here he sat in stupor, for how long?

He released her hands and stood. His eyes locked with hers as his body moved and bent over her chair. Restraint fled.

"I'm so in love with you." He touched her cheek and smiled. "May I kiss you?"

"Yes."

He pressed his lips to hers and rested one hand or her shoulder while the other steadied him at the table. Marjorie's arms enveloped his neck, and he felt her kiss in return. Neither broke the moment between them. Could his weak heart survive this intense happiness? How could he bear the intensity of his need to love, protect, and have her? He was, after all, flesh and bone.

Dadgum, they needed to breathe. She pulled away.

"Thank you." He touched her cheek.

"So, here we are," she shrugged, "two friends who've fallen in love."

"You were never my friend." He grinned and returned to his seat, noting that neither Jose nor the guitarist were anywhere in sight. Good men.

Marjorie must have noticed too. "Do you think we embarrassed our hosts?"

"Nope."

She reddened, becoming one with her dress.

Daniel's breath caught. They could not go back from what had just happened between them. For the second time in as many days, he knew exactly what he needed to do.

Now, how to make it happen? In a matter of seconds his brain compiled several possibilities, landing on the one he could accomplish the soonest. Trying to act nonchalant, in spite of his pounding heart, Daniel let Marjorie in on part of his plan.

"So, I think I mentioned to you my plan to do an art show in Austin, but it is on the same day as the dance." She nodded. "So, if I can pull myself away from you, I'm gonna go to Austin this weekend and visit the capitol even without doing an art show."

"Oh. What about your art class?"

"I'll cancel it."

"Going by yourself?"

"Yep."

No one needed to be with him when he picked out her engagement ring. He didn't know when he'd pop the question, but when the time was right, the ring would be waiting. He'd tour the capitol, so as not to be a liar, but only after he'd made a purchase from a jeweler in Austin. He didn't want her ring coming from the one fine jeweler in Hazel where he'd purchased one before.

"Sounds fun, Daniel. I'll miss you though."

"We'll go together sometime in the future."

"What would people think?"

"Let me be bold. At that point, maybe they'll think 'Daniel Buckler is taking his gorgeous wife on a weekend trip.'"

"Oh." She blushed, and his heart flip-flopped.

"I'll go to the church I attended in college, then come back Sunday afternoon and head straight to you, if that's okay."

"I might be taking a nap."

"I might know how to wake you up."

She blushed and smiled.

"I need to catch you up on some things, but not tonight."

She tilted her head. "Hum. You're a mystery."

Or an ignoramus for keeping quiet. He cleared his throat.

"I thought I made my feelings pretty clear a moment ago."

"We both did."

16

Marjorie propped her crutches beside the door and pulled it open. The Wright Do buzzed with activity for a late Saturday afternoon. *I love this place.* She'd be a daily fixture here if the school schedule allowed. For now, she relished her time on Mondays and Saturday afternoons. The concoction of shampoo and hair spray mixed with Valene's trade mark records formed a welcoming elixir.

With the crutches situated under her arms, Marjorie entered and blended with the hustle and bustle of the shop. Evelyn followed close behind, carrying two plates of brownies. Shoug sat under the dryer, ripping recipes from the latest innocent magazine. A woman occupied another dryer, her mouth slightly open with a snore escaping. Oh my! Marjorie recognized the lady who'd come a few weeks ago without her teeth.

"Marjorie," a lady called from the shampoo bowl where Valene lathered her hair. Her boss turned and offered a smile, a bit of relief evident by the way she glanced around the shop. Marjorie waved, then took note of who had called her name.

"Mrs. Darden, hi. It's good to see you." The woman's friendly acknowledgment gave Marjorie an extra spring in her otherwise hobbled step.

One of Valene's manicure customers bid hello as she stepped away from the table.

Gordon combed out the curls on one of his regulars. "Good to see you. Could you check my customer under the dryer?" He grinned.

"Should I wake her?" Marjorie chuckled.

"Only when it's time to come out from under the dryer. Won't do much good otherwise." He laughed. He addressed his client in the chair. "That's not to be repeated."

"Everyone, this is my friend from school, Evelyn. She wanted to see the shop." Marjorie explained as she moved toward the sleeping client.

"Welcome. I might put you to work." Valene raised her eyebrows, then paused long enough to swipe an errant strand of her own hair from her eyes.

Evelyn stopped following Marjorie and looked at Valene. "That'd be a blast."

"All right. How about checking on the laundry? Marjorie, can you set up my station, then take my next manicure? How's your foot?"

"Yes. And, getting better. Maybe I'll ditch the crutches on Monday."

"And, she brought brownies." Evelyn held out the plates covered in aluminum foil. "Where should I put these?"

Marjorie pointed to the small table between the waiting chairs. "Y'all indulge me and eat 'em up. It's my first attempt at homemade brownies." She turned toward Valene's station.

"Not so fast, young lady."

Marjorie startled at Valene's comment.

"How was your date?"

Wanda peeked at her from under a head full of suds. "Yes, we both want to know."

"And my wife wants to know." Gordon added.

"Me, too." Shoug spoke too loudly from beneath the dryer.

Seems the entire shop knew about her adventure.

"It was dreamy."

Words flowed from Marjorie as she shared almost all that Daniel had done to make their evening unforgettable. Her declaration of love and their kiss were no one else's business. Evelyn bragged on Marjorie's appearance, and the women responded with oohs and aahs.

"The man did good," Gordon remarked.

Yes. Yes, he did. Marjorie's thoughts had been on Daniel all day. My, how she hoped he enjoyed his tour. She wondered if he missed her as much as she missed him. Amazing how she felt a part of her was absent with him so far away.

Last night she'd dreamed they were married. Maybe his comment about her going to Austin triggered it. Husband and wife rolled down the highway in the red convertible while her wedding ring glistened in the sun. Her right hand rested on the open window and rode the wind.

"And how is Mrs. Buckler?"

"She's divine, Mr. Buckler."

They were one in every way God intended. She was no longer alone. He was hers and she was his.

"When is he back in town?" Wanda closed her eyes again as Valene sprayed water onto her shampooed hair.

Marjorie hoped her face didn't flush at the dream's memory. "Tomorrow night."

Aware of the busy reality, the beauty student prepped Valene's station for Mrs. Darden's set and style then began setting up the manicure table. An unfamiliar woman came into the shop and Valene directed her to Marjorie.

"I haven't met you. I'm Marjorie." She lifted the patron's arthritic fingers and settled them in the small bowl to soak.

"I'm Rosemary. I'm new here." Tears welled in the woman's eyes. Marjorie's heart tightened. This woman had left behind a life to come here. Marjorie had welcomed leaving her life behind to enter this community, while this woman likely grieved coming here.

"Welcome. I hope you feel at home very soon."

"I won't." And with that declaration, the patron's story gushed out. Marjorie listened, aware of the juxtaposition of their lives. Marjorie had been institutionalized at life's beginning, while this woman's large family had institutionalized her near life's end. No doubt, placing her at Hillhurst was in the lady's best interest, though she did not agree. Regret pushed itself forward in Marjorie's heart. She'd never understood her own "why," yet her parents must have thought the orphanage was in her best interest.

Motion at the door from the residential hall caught her eye, and Stewart entered, guiding Mr. Winkle inside the shop. Marjorie noted that her stomach didn't knot at his arrival; instead, a sense of appreciation came over her. As though he were looking for her, Stewart offered her a smile and nod before both his feet were through the doorway. Had he styled his hair differently? She squinted. No, but something about him had changed. Marjorie swallowed. The man appeared kind and warm to her. The source of the transition dawned on her. Stewart's appearance hadn't changed.

Her perception of him had. His words came to mind. "Give me another chance."

That's the least she could do for him. She'd reconsider her opinion of him as a person, but still not as a date. Who in this room had not been an awkward kid at some point? She certainly had.

Marjorie grinned. Evelyn's interest in the man felt right. She'd look forward to introducing them.

Marjorie focused on her customer, but she could hear Stewart settling Mr. Winkle in one of the waiting chairs.

"These brownies for me?" Stewart's inquiry drifted through the salon.

"Aren't we nosy?" Marjorie replied without looking his way. "Actually, one plate is yours for all your help the last couple of days. The others are to share."

She glanced up and saw him cram an entire brownie into his mouth as he sat down and took the *Windy Hop Tales* book from Mr. Winkle.

"I want her to read."

Mr. Winkle pointed at Marjorie.

"Go ahead. I can take over, if your boss doesn't mind." Evelyn had appeared from nowhere with absolute perfect timing and her entry had not gone unnoticed. Stewart's gaze zeroed in on her lovely companion. And his noticing had not gone unnoticed by Valene. Marjorie caught her looking at him in the mirror from her station.

"That's fine. Evelyn can take over." Valene smiled.

"Rosemary, my friend Evelyn will finish up."

She stood and washed her hands. "Stewart, this is my friend, Evelyn."

The man met her halfway and slid the book into her hands without so much as a glance, his eyes fixed on her friend now seated at the manicure table.

Marjorie sat down beside Mr. Winkle. "Which tale are we reading today?"

"The one about Grady the Grasshopper. He's my favorite."

"Mine too."

If Evelyn's bright eyes were any indication, Stewart charmed her by charming Rosemary, who blushed and smiled as he talked.

Life didn't always offer happy moments, but this was one, as Evelyn and Stewart were apparently at no loss for words.

Far happier were the moments last night, one after another, with Daniel.

My, my. Life was on a roll.

. . .

Marjorie would rather be sitting in any other food establishment than Rosie's right now. Evelyn had selected the diner when Stewart suggested they all grab a bite after the shop closed.

She sighed. Sure, the food tasted as delicious as always. And she didn't mind sitting next to Evelyn and across from Stewart. Oh, the irony of that truth. But all her Rosie memories included Daniel, who wasn't here. The place seemed deflated in his absence.

Don't be an idiot, Marjorie. The man can't be with you every moment of every day.

"Those twin sisters were a hoot at the shop today." Evelyn laughed as she lifted a fry to her mouth.

"Hillhurst is filled with stories of their audacity." Stewart grinned at Evelyn, and Marjorie stifled a chuckle. His eyes focused on her friend alone, and not her. How much difference a few hours could make. She might as well be a fly on the wall. Well, not in a diner.

Daniel would have laughed had he observed the last hour at the shop. "The sisters" from his art class had come in, and Shoug had taken the liberty to divulge details of their evening at the Mexican restaurant. Within moments, Marjorie clarified to the sisters that the night had not included a proposal as they assumed.

"Poor Gordon had his hands full." Stewart spoke only to Evelyn, his eyes lighting up every time she smiled, talked, or looked his way. "Neither sister would be still long enough for him to comb out their hair for styling. Seems they can't talk without bobbing their heads all over the place."

"Poor Gordon?" Marjorie lifted her left hand and pointed to it. "Poor Marjorie. I couldn't convince them no ring had been placed on my finger. They were certain I had simply forgotten to put it on."

"What woman would forget to put on her engagement ring?"

"Exactly, Evelyn. I hope they don't tell Daniel what they assumed next time they are in his class."

"Let's hope you see him first." Stewart's comment caused Marjorie to sit up straighter. Looking at her for the first time in several minutes, his eyes gleamed in a way that seemed supportive of her being with Daniel. Perhaps his romantic interest had found a permanent resting place in Evelyn.

Marjorie felt relieved, and somewhat comforted. It seemed Stewart's attention would not be on her. In fact, she could appreciate his good points.

"Oh, I have every intention of seeing Daniel before the sisters do." Marjorie flipped a strand of hair behind her ear. The action produced a subtle ache for the teacher.

As the evening moved on, the three of them fell into comfortable conversation. Marjorie relished hearing more about Evelyn's life and family. Even though Marjorie had spent most of her life envying every person who had a family, she didn't begrudge her friend. Nor had she begrudged Daniel his. In fact, he'd shared them with her as though her place had always been with them.

Her past might not have given her a loving home, but glimpses of her future seemed promising. She'd commit her life to Daniel the moment he asked—how she hoped he would ask. Then, in time, the two of them would offer their children a dream come true—two loving and nurturing parents. She could pray that God would give her the ability to be a good parent, though she lacked a decent role model.

My goodness. I better slow down my thinking. We've only just declared how we feel about one another.

"Marjorie can tell you. I was an awkward kid coming up." Stewart's large foot tapped her shin. He'd left her no choice but to respond.

"I told you Stewart had quite the crush on me when we were kids. One time..." She gentled her words. "Several times he made noble attempts to let me know."

Evelyn opened her mouth to reply, and a knot formed in Marjorie's stomach. She couldn't recall all she had told Evelyn about Stewart's bumbling pursuit of her. The last thing she wanted was a stupid comment to dampen any spark Stewart had for her friend. Evelyn's expression softened, and she looked directly at Stewart.

"I can hardly think on how I behaved as a kid in school. I was uncoordinated and way too corny. I wrote this guy a love poem, and he read it out loud at the lunch table. I wanted to die right then."

Marjorie offered Evelyn a balanced share of angst and sympathy over the traumatic experience. Her gratitude at the leveling statement went unspoken, but Evelyn's glance at her indicated she heard it.

Stewart glanced at Marjorie, then settled on Evelyn. "Maturity can polish rugged edges."

"Why, Stewart, that's profound." Marjorie nodded at the man across from her.

From the corner of the diner, a jukebox played a popular rock-and-roll song, and Evelyn sang along. Stewart joined her.

Marjorie could evaporate, and she suspected neither would miss her.

Daniel, on the other hand, better be missing her like crazy.

• • •

Last night common sense told Marjorie that Daniel wouldn't telephone her, yet she thumbed through the phone book trying to determine the cost of a long-distance call and if it were more than she reckoned he'd spend. Slurping the final bit of her coffee, she shut the book.

She uncrossed her legs and slid from the bed. One foot slipped into the fluffy, white house shoe that reminded her of Valene's cats. The other hovered inches from the floor while she grabbed her crutches. It was time to get ready for church and to stop obsessing over the lack of a telephone call from the man in Austin. Instead, she'd think about the fact that he was probably up and getting ready for church too.

Today she would sit in the singles Sunday School class alone, like most of its occupants, rather than alongside Daniel. She glanced at her reflection in the mirror as her toothpaste foamed up. She spit and rinsed. Being dubbed his girlfriend was not her concern today. Indeed, she'd have to appear as though his absence didn't occupy her thoughts. She could hold her own with the group of eight singles without much discomfort. She'd do anything to occupy the time while awaiting Daniel's return. Somehow when she'd made her tater-tot love declaration, a host of sleeping emotions awakened. She'd become half a person without him around. Possessiveness now played hide-and-seek inside her, peeking around corners at the thought of his time spent without her. She had to steady herself against a longing for him that threatened to knock her over.

Her life became marked by before tater-tot love and after it.

You lived in an orphanage? That was before.

You started beauty school? That was before.

You worried about being second-choice? That was before.

You can't function without him? That was after.

You're ready to walk the aisle? That was after.

She stared at herself in the mirror. "You're ready to open the envelope? That was after." The words were faint and Marjorie didn't know if she'd spoken them or thought them. Daniel's love and encouragement gave her courage to face her past. The person who had told Miss Bords she would never open the envelope had been a scared child, alone in the world. The person who now planned to open it was a mildly apprehensive woman with a supportive man cheering her on.

Daniel offered hope for her future and resolution with her past.

She swooped a brush through the ends of her hair, then sprayed the flipped ends. Tali's humming in the hallway as she waited her turn for the bathroom slipped beneath the door. Marjorie gave herself a once-over in the mirror before vacating the prime location.

She would open the envelope tomorrow and discover the truth of her past. Daniel had chosen her good, her bad, and her unknown. She'd done the same with him. She owed the same to herself. She and Daniel certainly didn't know everything about one another, but the heart knows what it knows. They belonged together.

If he proposed one day, the discovery of one another would be a lifelong journey.

Dressed and prepped, Marjorie opened the pink jewelry box Tali had loaned her. The plastic miniature ballerina no longer spun and the music no longer played, but she didn't mind. She appreciated the kind gesture from the young girl who had noticed she had no jewelry box of her own. The watch Daniel gave her rested at the bottom of the box, showing off against the light blue satin lining. She lifted it, kissed the small face, and clasped it on her wrist.

As she hobbled to the bedside table to grab a tissue and remove the lipstick her gesture had left on the watch, an idea struck her. She had fifteen minutes before the Bucklers would load up and head to church.

Just enough time to snoop.

She maneuvered to the closet and contorted herself enough to push a cardboard box with her toes. It felt light enough that she could push it all the way to her bed.

Why had she never sneaked a peek in this box before? She pulled open the flap that read "Daniel's room" and stifled a squeal when she saw the contents. The pennants, decor, and other items she'd seen in his room when she toured their house were stuffed on top of other items. Mrs. Buckler had done a meticulous job transforming the room into hers, but she wouldn't mind the pieces of Daniel's life still being displayed.

She looked at the painting on the wall beside the dresser. His unique signature seemed to smile at her from the corner of the art piece. Daniel was truly gifted. The piece was beautiful. Marjorie felt pleased that Lucy left it hanging when she redecorated.

Hum? Was her new habit of touching his signature when she left the room silly or romantic?

She laid the top items on the bed and lifted the object that piqued her curiosity. The fake leather on Daniel's senior yearbook seemed cold to the touch. She flipped through the pages until she found his picture. Adorable. The same childhood features she admired in the framed photograph down the Buckler hallway had morphed into the handsome senior smiling in black and white. He matured well, as she already knew.

She calculated back in time to determine what stage of life she was that same year. Strange how the person we will one day spend our life with moves and breathes unbeknownst to us until the life-altering moment that binds two hearts.

She flipped to the sports and activities sections, delighted each time she found his face.

She turned a page and gasped. Homecoming Queen and King. Her Daniel beamed at the queen while she beamed at the camera.

Candace. Young. Beautiful. Innocent of betrayal against the young man standing next to her.

Marjorie closed the book and hurried to get the items and box back in place. She slid her purse onto her arm, braced her Bible between her arm and chest, and paused at the painting before leaving the room.

Daniel the young boy didn't know her, but Daniel the man did, and he loved her. Just like in her case, his past no longer mattered.

. . .

The small Sunday School classroom felt nippy as Marjorie made her way to one of the metal seats forming a circle. One heel clicked against the tile in lopsided rhythm. She'd be glad to rid herself of these crutches and wear both her shoes again. The eclectic mixture of singles greeted her one after the other as she entered. A box of donuts, accompanied by paper cups and a pitcher of orange juice, rested on a crooked card table in the far corner. She paused when she recognized the person pouring herself a drink.

Candace.

She'd not been in the Sunday School class before. Why today?

The former homecoming queen turned, not looking the part of her senior role. Instead, she looked pale, and miserable. Marjorie wondered if the woman had a stomach bug again. She watched Candace sip the juice, then cringe before tossing the full cup into the trashcan. As Candace headed to the circle, her eyes locked with Marjorie's.

"What happened to your foot?" Inquiries from others mixed with Candace's question.

Marjorie shivered as she eased onto a cold metal chair and explained her night at the grocery store.

"Where's Daniel?" The man to her left looked around the room. Marjorie couldn't recall his name.

"He took a last-minute trip to Austin."

"Oh," Candace drawled, still standing behind another metal chair, "that must be why he canceled our plans. We were supposed to go out of town this weekend."

Words cannoned from Marjorie's mouth. "That's a lie."

Wasn't it? How had that thought slipped in?

Candace smirked. "Believe what you want. You barely know him. We have a history."

"Yes, and you betrayed it." Marjorie pursed her lips.

Someone in the circle spoke up, a man. Marjorie didn't know who, for her eyes remained fixed on Daniel's ex-fiancée.

"Candace," he insisted, "stop stirring up trouble. Kindly leave."

She did, in a huff, without a hint of kindness.

Marjorie closed her eyes and took a deep breath. The encounter unnerved her.

The atmosphere relaxed. The man spoke again. "Daniel is a good man. I won't hear lies about him." The class members offered their agreements.

Marjorie then glanced at the speaker and fought the urge to apologize for the scene. Instead, she voiced her own agreement.

"He is."

And she had to admit, a bit of relief set in with his affirmation. She hadn't misread Daniel.

• • •

"Ok. I'll see you in a few minutes." Marjorie hung up the telephone in the living room then noticed Tali's frown. She moved and stood next to her, then put her hand around the girl's shoulder. "Don't worry your pretty head about my leaving. I just feel like being at Evelyn's for a bit today." The girl offered a polite smile then spoke.

"I'm sorry Candace lied in front of the class this morning. I used to think she was this spectacular person. She's not."

"Maybe she will be spectacular again someday." *I doubt it right now.*

Lucy seated herself on the couch. "Tali, give me a minute with Marjorie." The girl squeezed Marjorie's waist in a slight hug of her own before walking out.

An awkwardness tightened Marjorie's muscles, and she found she couldn't look Lucy in the eyes. She gazed instead at the braided rug beneath the coffee table as she pushed words out her mouth.

"I didn't mean to bring all this tension about Candace into your home. Your family."

"Come sit."

Lucy patted the cushion beside her. Marjorie hobbled over and seated herself.

"You didn't bring this tension. Seems to me Candace would be wreaking havoc for Daniel no matter what. You are being dragged into it."

"Candace unnerved me today. I feel silly saying that out loud to you. I hope you don't mind my going to Evelyn's place."

"Your time is your own. And Candace has unnerved us all."

"I'll be back this evening." *Daniel and I need to talk.*

Lucy cleared her throat. "When I decided to rent a room, I didn't know who God would send our way. I just knew I wanted to help someone who had a need. Money was never a motive."

Marjorie smiled. *Obviously, because the monthly rent is barely more than I spent at the grocery store.*

Lucy continued. "When Daniel told us about this young woman he'd met who needed a place, I didn't know what to think. He has a good heart, and I wondered if that woman—you—might be trying to niggle your way into his life. He'd been hurt so badly by Candace. I didn't want him fooled again."

Marjorie sucked in a breath. She'd never considered they would need to examine her motive.

"But when I met you, and you cleared Leland's screening," she winked, "I had a peace."

"Thank you."

Marjorie tried not to panic, not knowing where the conversation was headed. Had Lucy lost that peace?

"I'm not naïve. I see the attraction between you and our son."

Marjorie would slither beneath that braided rug if she could. Lucy welcoming her into the home, including her with the family, and even helping her prepare for the date were one thing. Lucy acknowledging aloud the attraction between she and Daniel was another.

"You're blushing. Forgive me. All I am trying to say is that Daniel is a good man. You can trust him."

"I do."

But will Candace ever leave us alone?

17

Daniel beeped at his alma mater campus and waved as he drove by. If it were any other weekend in the past, he would stop, stroll the campus and snoop around the places where life had revolved for four years. But this was not any weekend in the past. This weekend was all about his future.

He drove past the capitol on his way out of the city with no hint of regret over cramming a full afternoon visit to the building into an hour. By the time he'd gone to his bank for money, driven to Austin, and made his selection at the jeweler, there was no time for a leisurely stroll of the grounds and ornate building yesterday. Assuming Marjorie would ask him about the capitol, he'd slipped inside and refreshed his memory of the layout and unique details.

Though he enjoyed seeing a few familiar faces this morning at his college church, he'd felt somewhat out of joint without Marjorie beside him. He imagined himself the student assigned to the last seat on the one row in his classroom that had an extra desk. He'd have to rearrange his seating on Monday. No one needed to feel out of joint.

His eyes roamed to the passenger seat where a velvet box rested. He'd spent every bit of dough he'd brought, except enough for meals and the lined box, on the engagement ring and matching wedding band. The set was out of this world, if he said so himself. His savings account took a hit, but for the past two years, he'd been fattening that account because he'd lived a simple, but good, life that didn't require much beyond the basics. He looked into the bright sky and thanked God for his convertible that his dad passed to him and for his house. God's blessings had set him up for this fresh start on life. If he were able to paint his gratitude to its deepest extent, the piece would be museum-worthy.

He didn't know when he would propose to Marjorie, but he did know he wouldn't prolong the wait. Decorum might dictate a traditional Christmas proposal. He could care less about that type of decorum at the moment.

He had 246 miles to think on the when and how.

Daniel blew out a breath. As much as he loved Marjorie, he didn't know the intricacies of her heart in the matter of being orphaned. He wondered if even she could know her heart until the truth was revealed.

Lord, prepare Marjorie for the news in the envelope.

He shifted in his seat.

Another thing he knew was that he had to tell Marjorie about the matter with Candace.

Had he been a coward not telling her Friday night?

He had not wanted to spoil their date, but something nagged at him.

Had his intentions for waiting been selfish? Sitting behind the wheel now with his future tucked into a velvet jewelry box beside him, the answer revealed itself. Yep, he'd been selfish.

He pressed harder on the gas pedal. He couldn't get home soon enough.

. . .

Daniel tucked his treasured purchase behind the socks in his drawer, then snatched it back. That's how he had stored the ring for Candace.

Nope, Marjorie's ring belonged somewhere else. He glanced around his room, his gaze landing on the perfect spot. He opened the narrow drawer of his bedside table and scooted his Bible to the right before tucking the jewelry box next to it. The location was symbolic—next to God's Word.

The bundle of mail he'd yanked from his box lay on his dresser. He picked it up and started to thumb through it, then tossed it back where it landed face down. Good grief. The mail could wait.

With a last glance in the bathroom mirror and a pat of after-shave on his cheeks, he scurried back to his convertible. Time to see Marjorie.

Though the air felt brisk and cutting, he couldn't resist the clear sky. He opened up the top and backed onto the street. Marjorie would be staring upward in admiration if she were seated next to him. And he would stare in admiration at his view too.

His mind wondered to the telephone call he'd made to Conrad. The man's response surprised him. He had no idea if yesterday Candace aborted a child or if Conrad tried to mend a marriage. *God, help them.*

He pulled out of the subdivision and hit the main road. Within moments, he stood outside the Buckler home where his lady awaited. He threw the car into park and trotted to the front porch.

The screen door revealed his dad and Lucy engrossed in a television show. He pulled on the door handle and let himself in.

"Hello."

His parents startled.

"Daniel." Lucy stood to greet him while his dad walked over and shut off the television.

"Did you have a good trip?" His step-mom offered a smile, but her brow wrinkled.

"Great trip. Where's everybody else?"

"Well, Theo is down the street. Tali is playing records in her room." Lucy's hands fidgeted with the hem of her blouse.

His dad stood and turned off the television and sat back down. "Rusty is still in the hospital, by the way."

Daniel studied his father. Why had the man inserted that piece of information before either of them told him Marjorie's whereabouts? Admittedly, he had wondered about Rusty, but it was not forefront in his mind.

"That's too bad. Where's Marjorie?"

Silence.

"Marjorie!" He moved toward the hallway to fetch her from the bedroom. His father's hand tugged his shoulder, and Daniel stilled.

"She's not here."

Not here?

Was she not anxious to see him? Something urgent must have come up.

"Where is she?"

"At her friend Evelyn's house." His father grimaced.

"When will she be back?"

"This evening."

He noticed his step-mother, silent during the dialogue, frowning. Friend? Surely, she wasn't as disappointed as he was that Marjorie was not here to meet him.

Something akin to devastation coursed through his veins. Whatever hadn't been said yet would likely alter his life—again.

Wait. Maybe the reason wasn't life-altering. Maybe Evelyn needed Marjorie for some reason. There had to be a reasonable explanation.

"Sit, Son." The words came from his step-mother.

Daniel backed onto the edge of the chair.

"Why are you two so ambiguous?" His words sliced the air.

"Candace came to your Sunday School class today." The lawyer in his father spoke the statement. Daniel knew the tone—Leland Buckler was honing in on a point no jury could deny.

Daniel's head dropped.

"Did you tell Marjorie about Candace and the baby? That you called Conrad?"

His head moved side to side. "Not yet. Did Candace tell her?"

"No."

Whew.

"Please get to the point, Dad."

"Candace announced that your sudden trip to Austin must be why you canceled plans to go out of town with her yesterday."

Anger, regret, and loss formed a hideous groan that spewed out his throat. No, no, no. What a fool he'd been to think Candace would do the right things—not get an abortion, which she must not have, and leave Marjorie alone, which she hadn't.

That woman had morphed into pure evil.

And he had morphed into pure ignorance.

Lucy spoke up. "Marjorie said she stood up for you. The class did too. Candace was asked to leave. But the whole encounter unnerved Marjorie. So, she called Evelyn after lunch and went there."

She dreads facing me. The thought burdened him.

"Did y'all explain things to her?"

His father lowered his head. "We wanted to, but that is your responsibility."

"You're right. But you could have spared her some agony."

"You could have too, Son," his stepmother added.

How had Marjorie held it together in Sunday School? Oh, why, why, why had he left her all alone, unguarded without the truth. He should have driven home Saturday night. He should have risked telling her Friday.

"Where? Do you know where Evelyn lives?"

Lucy startled at his loud voice.

"No. And no telephone number, but Candace said she'd be back this evening."

"I gotta find her before then."

Daniel fled to his car, the screen door slamming behind him. Just as he pulled open the convertible's door, his stomach revolted, tossing his food and his emotions into a mess on the ground.

His mind raced to determine who might know Evelyn's address or telephone number.

No one came to mind.

And with that realization, Daniel lost his.

No amount of driving all over town, chewing pencils, or staring at the wedding ring set could fix his problem this moment.

He would have to wait a lifetime for this evening.

18

Marjorie tapped her foot to the beat from music being played in the apartment next door as she pulled the hot pan of brownies from the oven in Evelyn's yellow kitchen. The walls were thin in this complex she hadn't even looked at because it offered no furnished units. How interesting to see her friend's flair for decorating. Her entire abode boasted bright yellow walls with the furniture, curtains, and knick-knacks popping against it in bold shades of orange, purple, green, and blue. The mid-afternoon sun added its own brightness through the kitchen window.

"I love your place. You've got style."

"Thanks. My mother is a decorator for a company that caters to the Dallas wealthy. She gets most of the credit for this place. Yum, the brownies smell delicious."

"Nothing like chocolate to calm the nerves. Let's eat."

Evelyn poured them both a glass of milk while Marjorie cut into the warm dessert and served them each a piece. The first bite sizzled on her tongue.

"Thanks for letting me crash here this afternoon."

"Glad you telephoned and asked to come. Care to talk more about what's up?"

Marjorie sighed and fought back tears.

"After Candace's escapade I told you about, I felt so out of sorts with the Bucklers. Like, who am I kidding? Their son almost married Candace. And here I am thinking I'll be their daughter-in-law soon. I felt ridiculous."

Evelyn took a sip of milk. "Well, I don't know the Bucklers, but if I had to guess by the look on Mrs. Buckler's face when I came to pick you up, I'd say she looked sad, maybe even worried, that you felt the need to get away."

"Mrs. Buckler told me in so many words that she was glad I was living there. And that I could trust Daniel."

"Interesting. And bold."

"Yes." Marjorie blushed. She'd keep the details of Lucy's conversation to herself.

"It's none of my business, but no telling what Daniel will think if he goes to his parents before you get back."

"It hurts me to think about that. But I needed time away from anything about Daniel. I'll explain to him later and hope he understands."

"Do you trust Daniel?"

"Yes. But I don't like Candace's shenanigans."

"But he says he's over her."

"She's not over him."

"Do you think he really had plans with her this weekend?"

"No!"

Marjorie felt certain of that fact because her gut told her Daniel wasn't a liar or two-timer. But what she wasn't certain about was what motivated Candace to state otherwise. Something else picked at her as well. Daniel's decision to go to Austin felt hasty, as though he'd planned it on the spot when he told her. Maybe it was nothing more than the man she confessed falling in love with had an impulsive side to him.

"Evelyn, I didn't mean to sound rude. I guess I just felt strongly that Candace was lying."

"Talk to Daniel."

"Did I ever tell you about the envelope I have from the orphanage?"

With that Marjorie steered the conversation toward another topic all about her.

. . .

Marjorie hugged her friend before getting out of her car. Evelyn drove off, beeping and waving out the window—at Daniel.

The man was seated on the front steps at his parents' house. She'd watched him sit up from his slumped position at the sound of the car pulling in, but remained seated, looking her direction while offering Evelyn a wave in return. What was the man thinking?

Marjorie pulled off her sunglasses and placed them in her purse. Her eyes never strayed from Daniel as she hobbled through the yard toward him. Oh my. She loved this man. Not one ounce of doubt about that.

"Hi." She pushed a strand of hair behind one ear.

"Hi." Daniel replied as he slid to one side of the step.

She set her purse on the step above them before sitting beside him and leaning her crutches against the step. "How was your trip?"

He reached and pulled the tucked hair from behind her ear. The strands brushed her cheek before settling into place. His gesture felt intimate.

"It was good, but I missed you." His hand clasped hers.

She believed him. "I missed you too. How long have you been here?"

"A couple of hours."

"I'm sorry I wasn't here."

A second of awkwardness sat between them.

"Marjorie, about Candace."

Tears welled in her eyes then rolled down her cheeks. She wiped them with her free hand.

"She was in Sunday School class today and made quite an announcement about you."

"I heard. I am so sorry you had to deal with that."

"Why did you go to Austin, Daniel?"

"To buy you an engagement ring."

She sucked in a breath.

"I didn't plan to tell you. But I've made a mess of things, and I figure you needed to hear that truth before I explain myself."

He bought me a ring? Her head spun over his declaration.

"I've never lied to you, Marjorie, about Candace or anything else. I even stopped by the capitol so I could tell you I went there." She felt her lips spread in a smile.

"But there is something about Candace I should have told you before I left instead of waiting."

Her emotions twitched.

"What?"

Words gushed from his mouth about a pregnancy and an abortion and moral confusion and a phone call to Conrad. Images of Candace looking pale and puny paraded across her mind. The puzzle pieces fit together.

"I didn't want to ruin our special date night, but not telling you sooner is one of the most stupid decisions of my life."

Marjorie's mind replayed the dreamy evening at the Mexican restaurant. Knowing what she knew now, would she have wanted Daniel to tell her then? Tenderness toward his dilemma set in.

"You had to make a judgment call. I get it."

"You do? I'm not sure I deserve that from you."

"You do. What did Conrad say when you told him about the pregnancy?"

"He knew about it. Said it wasn't his. She obviously had an affair."

Marjorie gasped. "Can he prove that?"

"He can't have children, he told me." She watched Daniel's face heat at that statement. Hers heated as well. *Maybe Daniel should have skipped that detail.*

"He loves her. Said he didn't break up our friendship for nothing. Wants to raise that baby as his own."

"Then why did she leave him?"

"I don't know. He really doesn't either. But he is coming to Hazel to try and get her back." Daniel glanced at his watch. "Probably here already."

"Oh."

"Remember I told you he telephoned me?"

"Yes."

"He was wanting to me know. To warn me she would likely lie about their relationship." Daniel squeezed her hand. "If I hadn't been so hotheaded, I would have known and could tell Candace I knew, and maybe, somehow, she would have left me—us—alone. I can't believe I even considered whether I had a responsibility toward helping that unborn baby."

"Your heart is good, Daniel."

"A good thing unguarded can become a weakness."

She touched his cheek. "Mr. Buckler, you are wise."

"Not so. Just determined to learn from my mistakes. Will you forgive my poor judgement?"

"There is nothing to forgive."

Daniel touched his forehead to hers. "Thank you. I love you, Marjorie."

"I love you, too."

Peace and satisfaction filled her. *Now, about that ring?*

He pulled away and grinned at her. "So, for now, can you forget that I blurted out about the ring?"

The man was a mind reader.

"Impossible."

"I figured. Did I waste my money?"

"Only if you keep the ring to yourself."

"Impossible."

"How's the foot?"

"Going without crutches tomorrow."

"Cool. Wanna go to Rosie's tomorrow night?"

"Yes."

Daniel stood and pulled her up. Good, because her bottom had gone numb.

"For now, could you help me get in good standing with my family? I'm kind of in the dog house."

"You're still irreplaceable to them."

"How about to you?"

"Absolutely"

19

Gordon offered a quiet greeting Monday morning as Marjorie closed the door from the parking lot.

"Where's Valene?"

"At the hospital with Wanda."

"What happened?" She blurted the question.

"Wanda had emergency surgery late last night. Her gallbladder burst."

"Oh, my goodness. Is she okay?"

"Valene said she has a long recovery ahead."

Marjorie prepared the shampoo bowls and manicure table as Gordon explained the plan for the day. In Valene's absence, he would do the cuts and styling. Marjorie would do shampoos, manicures, and some of the rolling.

"Your friend Evelyn agreed to come do laundry and clean up."

Evelyn? Yesterday afternoon her friend hadn't mentioned a thing about coming.

The door from the residential hall squeaked, and Marjorie looked up. Stewart held the door open for Evelyn, then followed her through.

"Surprised?" Evelyn winked at her.

"Yes. And happy you're here."

"Stewart telephoned me last night and asked if I could come help. And since the beauty school is closed on Mondays, I decided why not come here and learn again by watching and helping."

"I picked her up and am delivering her to you. I asked Valene first, and she said absolutely." Stewart grinned at his companion. Marjorie found his gesture amusing since Evelyn owned a car.

Evelyn and Stewart reiterated their already-agreed-upon lunch plans, then Stewart headed off for work. His merry whistling followed him out the door and down the hallway. Marjorie allowed a small smile to form on her lips. They must have hit it off more than she realized the other night at Rosie's. Evelyn hadn't given a hint of increased interest last night.

Preannounced by her perfume, Evelyn sidled up to Marjorie. "You hangin' in there?"

Marjorie placed some bobby pins onto Valene's station and took Evelyn's hands.

"I am. Daniel and me had a talk. We're good." *He has a ring!* "And I'm horribly selfish for not even asking you about Stewart yesterday."

"You're asking now." Evelyn squeezed her fingers.

"I'm so happy for you. I want details."

"We've got a busy day ahead, ladies." Gordon's chide oozed with kindness. "And we have to close early with Valene out," he continued. "I have a personal obligation this afternoon."

Marjorie hugged Evelyn. "I'm glad you're here."

Four hours into the day, Marjorie sat at the small table in the back room and stared at the sandwich she'd packed. Her foot throbbed. She rubbed her forehead with her fingers, but a headache persisted, as though it were sympathetic to her aching foot. The first day without crutches had been tough. She blew out a breath, then forced a bite of sandwich down her throat. Perhaps some food would help. She scooted her chair back and opened the door.

"Does anyone have aspirin?"

Gordon caught her eye in the mirror. "Valene keeps a bottle in her top desk drawer."

Marjorie headed to the supply room that Valene called an office, but hearing Shoug Jennings' recognizable voice, she turned back toward the front of the salon as the sweet lady entered. Stewart held the door with one hand and his lunch box with the other. He eased by the pie lady and headed to Evelyn, who was sweeping up hair.

Shoug walked toward Marjorie with a pie in her hand. "I have a treat for Daniel." She shoved the pie at her. "I heard he cancelled his class today." *He did?* "Please give him his pie."

Shoug turned her attention toward Gordon. "You ready for me?"

Marjorie shrugged. "Thanks." Why had he cancelled? And how would they meet up for Rosie's? Or would they meet up?

As the day wound down, Marjorie and Evelyn handled the last bit of clean up and laundry as Gordon rushed off to wherever it was he had to be. Stewart entered the shop. "My shift is over. Ready for dinner, Evelyn?"

"Sure am. I'm starving."

Marjorie hugged her friend. "Thanks for everything." Then she spoke in a whisper, "I want Stewart scoop tomorrow in class."

Evelyn whispered in return. "You betcha. And I want Daniel scoop tomorrow too."

. . .

Marjorie watched Stewart and Evelyn leave together, then stood in the center of the shop feeling foolish. The plan had been to meet Daniel in his art classroom down the hall, but he'd cancelled class, according to Shoug. She reckoned she'd take a bus back to the Bucklers. The truth was, at this moment, she didn't know how much more of Daniel's impulsiveness or mystery, or whatever it is, she could take.

She glanced in the mirror at Valene's station. "Are you a fool?" Her reflection didn't answer, but Doubt shouted. "Maybe I really was his second choice, and he's having a hard time. Maybe he forced himself to buy a ring to convince his own heart he was ready for another woman. I'm nothing but a gullible, vulnerable little girl in an adult body."

The door creaked, interrupting Doubt, and Marjorie stopped staring at herself as she saw Daniel step into the shop.

"Hey. Whew, have I told you how pretty you look in uniform?"

"Hi." *Yes, I totally ignored your compliment because I'm flustered.*

Daniel's eyebrows wrinkled. "Where's everyone?"

"The shop closed early." She threw out a hasty explanation of the day's events.

"I had no idea about any of that. Poor Wanda."

Marjorie shifted to ease the pain of her foot. Daniel moved to steady her. "Your foot. How was the first day without crutches?"

"Not bad. Well, ok. My foot hurts." She shifted to free her arm from his support.

"Shoug brought you a pie. It's in the laundry room refrigerator. She said you cancelled your class."

"Ah, ha. I was just coming to tell you about that." He closed the gap between them. "I cancelled because I made other plans for us tonight besides Rosie's, if you don't mind."

She mentally kicked Doubt out the door.

"No." She grinned. "Do they involve food, because I'm hungry."

"Food is involved. But, I'm not quite ready. Can you hang out here another half hour?"

"Ok. I've got homework anyway."

"I'll be back." The man turned on his heels and left the shop.

Marjorie smiled. This kind of mystery she could take.

True to his word, Daniel returned within the half hour and led her down the hall, supporting her weight.

"Are we eating in the dining room here?"

He laughed, "Not a chance." A little further down the hall, he paused. Marjorie knew immediately where they were.

"I cancelled class because I have a private sitting in here tonight to start a portrait I booked at the last minute."

"Oh, do I get to watch you paint?"

"If you don't mind. If you do, I can reschedule the sitting."

"I'd love to watch."

He opened the door. A blank canvas sat on an easel front and center in the room. A chair was positioned behind it. The scent of burgers filled the air, and her stomach responded.

"Who are you painting?"

He grinned. "A beauty school student."

Her skin smiled with goose bumps. "You're going to paint my picture?"

"If you'll let me. I'd like to start on it tonight, but I won't get finished."

She clasped both hands under her chin. "I've never hardly had a picture taken of me. This is exciting."

The satisfaction on his face thrilled her.

"Good. After we eat." He nodded toward the burgers laid out on a nearby card table.

Daniel blessed the food then Marjorie popped a tot into her mouth and hurried to chew. "So," she swallowed, "how long will it take to paint?"

"Two or three months. We'll go about an hour tonight so you can get a feel for things, then we'll schedule other sittings. I wanted to start here but will end up painting it at home." Daniel ran a napkin over his mouth.

"So do I just sit real still while you paint?"

He chuckled. "Yes."

"Maybe you could play some of your classical music. I'd like that."

"Beethoven it is." She noticed him shift in his seat.

"Marjorie, have you given more thought to opening the envelope?"

"Honestly, not in a day or so. My mind was on other things, but I won't say her name."

"Right."

She set her burger on the wrapper and took a sip of cola. The two of them had worked through the confusion of the weekend, and she had to admit that the envelope had been on her mind until Candace appeared on Sunday. She sighed.

"Tonight. I'll open it tonight."

"I didn't mean to pressure you."

"No. It feels right to me. I'm ready to learn whatever my parents thought I should know. I'm weary of wondering. It's time to move on."

. . .

To calm her nerves, Marjorie crumpled the note she'd found on the coffee table in the Buckler's den. They had gone to some neighbors for dinner. Daniel seemed to linger on his parents' porch where they had gone to say goodbye. Perhaps he was hesitant to walk away from her, thinking she might need him as she learned the truth about herself tonight. However, she knew that coming to terms with her past had to be done on her own terms. And for her, that meant being alone.

"Daniel, I promise to call you if I need to."

"I can sleep here on my parents' couch. Wouldn't that be better than a phone call?"

Marjorie opened the screen door, trying to indicate it was best if he left. He reached over and kissed her forehead.

"I'll be praying for you. At home. Can I call you tomorrow night?"

"Yes. And I'll tell you everything."

With that, he turned and walked down the porch steps.

"The painting is looking fantastic. If I say so myself."

He looked over his shoulder. "Thank you. The subject inspires me."

Marjorie bit her lip then slipped inside the empty house. She scribbled a note to the Bucklers wishing them a good night and that she'd see them in the morning. Once inside Daniel's old room— her room—she went to the dresser and opened the drawer where she kept the envelope. Lifting her pajamas, she pulled them from the drawer along with the envelope. With trembling hands, she placed the envelope on the edge of the bed before preparing for the night's rest—if she got any after what she would discover. Once she dressed for bed, Marjorie piddled around straightening her dresser top, checking for clean towels, and blowing dust from the bedside table.

With nothing left to do but stall, Marjorie situated herself in the middle of the bed. Her spirit tugged. "Dear God, I'm scared. But you already know what's inside, so help me be brave. And thank you for Daniel, who cares."

She pulled up the silver clasp of the envelope, then slid her finger under the flap to loosen it. Her fingers widened the mouth. She gasped.

Various envelopes were stuffed inside. She turned the manila envelope over and let the contents fall onto the bedspread. In the midst of the contents, a small drawstring bag landed next to her knee.

Her fingers trembled as she picked up one of the aged letters. It had been opened years before. XOXOXO was written across the bottom in a heavy hand. She flipped the envelope over.

Her past nearly suffocated her.

"It can't be."

She pulled it to her lips so the return address pressed against them. Perhaps his scent lingered in the papers. She kissed the envelope, then pulled it away to stare. The name tingled on her lips.

"Pvt. Troy Darden"

20

Marjorie yawned as she walked down the hall toward the beauty school bathroom Tuesday morning. The door was cracked open, and she could see Evelyn teasing her hair with a rat tail comb. The two of them were always early arrivals to school. Class wouldn't start for another twenty minutes.

"Good morning." She tapped on the door with her knuckle. Evelyn must have seen her through the mirror, for she dropped the comb. It clinked in the sink.

Her friend squealed. "You had a good date last night. I can see it on your face. You're smiling, and your eyes are bright."

"Yes, I did. Daniel started painting my portrait."

"How romantic."

"It is. Oh, Evelyn, you won't believe it when I tell you what else happened. You just won't believe it."

She watched Evelyn's eyes dart to her left hand.

"Oh, my. Not that."

"What then? Tell me. I am about to burst with curiosity."

Marjorie was on the verge of bursting as well. She had to tell someone that she'd learned about her past.

"I opened my envelope."

Evelyn leaned against the sink. "Can you tell me what you learned?"

She clasped her friend's hands. "I will, but sorry, there are two people I need to tell before anyone else knows."

She inserted dramatic pause.

"First, Daniel."

"Daniel! You're related to Daniel?"

"No. Not yet, anyway." Marjorie freed her left hand and wiggled the empty ring finger. "But someday."

"Does he know any of your story?"

"Not yet. He knows I was planning to open the envelope after he left last night. He's supposed to call me tonight, and I'll tell him."

"Uhm, who else do you need to tell?"

"That has to stay a secret for now."

"Understood. I'm proud of you. And so happy that it was apparently good news."

"It was good. And surprising." Marjorie bounced on her toes then bit her tongue. She better change the subject or she'd spill the entire story.

"Are you seeing Stewart tonight?"

"No. He has to drive to his real home in Waxee. Something about helping his dad with a project. I'll miss him."

"Tell me all about it."

As the two of them made their way to the classroom, her friend chatted away about the man who sounded nothing like the boy version of himself Marjorie had known.

"I'm going to church with him next week. Do you think Methodists allow Presbyterians in their churches?"

Marjorie laughed as she situated herself at the desk and opened her textbook to the next chapter. "Why wouldn't they?"

"If you're not seeing Daniel tonight, do you want to hang out at my place?"

"I'm going to the hospital."

"Why are you going to the hospital?"

"To visit Wanda Darden."

"You'd visit Mrs. Darden instead of spending time with Daniel? I think you've gone looney."

Marjorie. "Yep." She enjoyed her friend's confusion.

Evelyn shrugged and opened her own textbook.

Within seconds, her friend leaned into her ear and spoke, her voice much too loud for Marjorie's comfort and saturated with awareness. "Wanda Darden? Marjorie, I can't believe that you're related to her!"

Evelyn was a smart girl.

. . .

Marjorie rose from the desk and stretched her back. Peers who would be working the Dance Do stepped away from their desks too. The college administrator flipped her notepad closed. "Good meeting, ladies. I think we've made good plans for the Dance Do." Marjorie agreed. Still a month away, the event was promising to be a success.

She hugged Evelyn. "See you later."

"Not so fast. I'm dropping you off at the hospital."

What a good friend.

Once she was situated in Evelyn's car, Marjorie pulled a small drawstring bag from her purse.

"What's that?"

"Jewelry. My mom left it to me." She lay the bag on the envelope in her lap.

"Oh, that brings tears to my eyes."

"I sure cried when I saw them." Marjorie adorned herself with the items. She touched the small pearl hanging from a silver chain around her neck and glanced at the new-to-me watch. Contentment filled her insides.

More than once today she regretted telling Evelyn any bit of news about her past before the people who most needed to know heard it. But she couldn't take back her actions. She'd considered calling Daniel this morning. She'd considered telling the Bucklers. In the end, she'd decided to relish the news all on her own.

Except she hadn't. Sort of.

Evelyn pulled the car into the hospital parking lot.

"Thanks for the ride. You're a good friend." Marjorie opened the door then hesitated. She turned back to Evelyn. "Thanks for listening today..."

Evelyn finished her thought. "Don't worry. I won't tell anyone your news. Good friends can be trusted."

Marjorie nodded her head up and down in agreement, then got out of the car.

"Remember to telephone me when it's time to bring you home. No need to ride the bus."

Marjorie waved. "Ok."

Evelyn rolled up her window then puttered out of the hospital parking lot.

Marjorie had never been inside the hospital. Chalk it up to good health and the orphanage clinic. Much about it reminded her of Anderson Orphanage and Hillhurst. She hugged the envelope close and stopped at the reception area.

"Mrs. Darden is located down the first hall on the right. Room 124. Visitation ends in two hours."

Marjorie smiled and thanked the attendant, then headed toward the hall. Her ankle was doing surprisingly well. As she neared the hallway, a voice called her name. Goosebumps tingled her skin, and her heart sped up.

The man she loved was here. Marjorie turned to find him exiting the hall on the left, a man and woman following him out the door. "Daniel." She moved toward the trio, aware that the last time Daniel had seen her, she had wanted to be alone. Not anymore.

"Hi."

He tilted his head, a wrinkle furrowing on his brow.

"Hi. What are you doing here?"

"Visiting Wanda. How about you?"

"Visiting Rusty." He finally released a grin. "Folks, this is Marjorie Mullins. We..."

The man, whom she didn't know, interrupted. "So, you must be the Marjorie that our Curtis has talked about."

Now it was Marjorie's brow that wrinkled.

Daniel blurted, "These are the Channings—Curtis' parents. We ran into one another in Rusty's room."

The woman stepped closer to Marjorie. "Forgive us. Curtis has talked about Mr. Buckler's girlfriend who is..." She bit her lip.

"An orphan." Marjorie felt sorry for the couple and wished them relief from the awkwardness.

"Well, this is an awful introduction, but once Curtis learned that you were an orphan, he became fixated on you."

Creep.

"What my wife is trying to say is that last spring we told Curtis that we had adopted him."

Daniel reacted with a slight gasp.

"He didn't take it too well. I think his bad behavior this year is his acting out about the truth."

Marjorie's heart tendered. "Being orphaned is a tough situation, no matter how good life may be. So, if you like, maybe we can all talk together sometime over supper. It might be helpful to him or you. "

She looked at Daniel. "I'm sure Mr. Buckler wouldn't mind working out a time."

"Not at all."

The couple agreed, then bid their good -byes.

Before Daniel could start questioning her, she grabbed his hand and pulled him toward a back door she'd spotted.

"I've got so much to say to you." The words seemed to bounce with her lopsided stride.

They stood just outside the back doors. She held his hand while the other grasped her envelope. He nodded toward it.

"Did you read it?"

"Yes."

"And you brought it here?"

"Yes."

She stared into his eyes, desiring to connect with his soul. He leaned forward and kissed her cheek.

Their love for one another seemed to heat the brisk evening air. As though he felt it too, Daniel stepped back.

"Are you okay?"

"Yes."

"What did you find in the envelope?"

She rocked on her toes. "Daniel, you won't believe it."

He laughed, and his joy warmed her heart.

"You've got to come with me to Wanda's room."

"Why?"

"Because of the envelope." She pecked his cheek and tugged his arm, but he stood in place.

"You're mysterious."

"The opposite. I'm full of news."

He kissed her cheek again. *The lips. Kiss the lips, Daniel.*

He clasped her hand, and the warmth and fit of it made her feel whole. The news in the envelope somersaulted in her head. She had a past, and a pretty awesome present. The thought of her future seemed more than she could contain.

"Mr. Buckler, sir, can a person explode from happiness?"

He cleared his throat. "Well, that's a good question, Miss Mullins. Since I am not a science teacher, my answer is speculation. I would say no, it can't."

"Then I'm not sure what's happening inside me."

"The heart shapes itself around the emotions the soul feels."

"That's a good answer, Mr. Buckler."

"I know this from experience."

He paused in the hallway.

"Can I ask you a question?"

"Yes."

"How do you plan to get home tonight?"

"You, of course."

Just as they reached Wanda's room, Daniel stopped and turned her to face him. "Even though I don't know yet what's in the envelope, I can assume it involves Wanda, and I assume it is good news. But either way..."

He paused.

"Either way, it may be more than her heart can handle right now. She's sick and weak."

Marjorie's excitement stilled and her stomach dropped, but Daniel's thoughts were something to consider. She had just buried her son's body, after years of it missing. To learn he'd fathered a child might add to her heartbreak.

Even if the child lived and worked around her.

"I hadn't thought about that. Let's still see her, though, since we are here."

"Maybe you should tell Valene the news first and let her prepare Wanda."

Marjorie imagined Valene easing Mrs. Darden into the news. She had a way with the woman.

"That's also a good idea."

"I hope I haven't burst your bubble."

"Maybe a little, but you're right. My news could be too much for her in her condition. But no matter what, you will hear the news tonight."

"I can't wait to hear it."

Daniel tapped on the hospital door and Marjorie recognized Valene's voice, "Come in."

She slipped in ahead of him, and cold chills ran over her. Her hand moved instinctively to her mouth, and her eyes stung as tears threatened to form. Wanda appeared to be in a deep sleep with wires everywhere.

Marjorie turned wide eyes toward her boss.

"She's on medication to help her sleep."

Daniel eased next to Marjorie, and Valene's eyebrows raised.

"Your crutches are gone."

"Yes. Now I hobble all on my own."

Marjorie moved to the bedside. "Hello, Mrs. Darden. It's Marjorie. Daniel and me are here to see you."

The face that had offered rebukes and some kindnesses looked worn and aged. Marjorie glanced at Wanda's fingers, then touched her trademark manicure. She rested inside that body, somewhere.

"Valene, do you need a break? We can sit with her for a bit." Daniel's offer sounded appropriate and kind.

"No thanks. Truth is, they said she won't wake up anymore tonight, so I thought I'd go home and get cleaned up."

"How did the shop go today?" Marjorie had wondered all day long.

"Gordon rescheduled or canceled most of my appointments for today and tomorrow."

"I wish I could help out more."

"Gordon said you and Evelyn were a great help."

Daniel spoke up, "Can I take you two ladies to Rosie's?"

Valene didn't answer, but instead pointed to the envelope.

"Is that from the orphanage?"

Marjorie jerked. Good thing Wanda wasn't alert, or they'd all be in an awkward situation.

"Yes."

"Is it good news?"

"Yes. You won't believe it. I want to share the news with you sometime soon."

Valene looked directly at Daniel. "I'd like a meal at Rosie's while I hear good news. Unless this is too soon for Marjorie."

"It's not."

"We've got a deal, ladies."

Marjorie gasped. "I need to telephone Evelyn and let her know you'll bring me home. She dropped me off."

"Let's do that while Valene says her goodbyes."

She and Daniel moved toward the hall.

"Meet us at the reception area." Marjorie whispered, then shut the door.

• • •

Daniel rubbed a hand over his nervous stomach after he settled Marjorie in the passenger seat and closed the door. The sensation took him by surprise. He wasn't expecting his own set of nerves over the envelope's contents.

He loved Marjorie so much he ached. The thought that she'd had to work through a multitude of varying emotions over the last few days caused his own inward battle. He regretted his role in the negative feelings but was thankful that he was able to experience the apparent good ones with her.

He crossed the front of his car and glanced at her. Wrapped in his jacket, she looked so delicate.

And beautiful.

He pulled out of the hospital parking lot and made sure Valene followed him. He'd realized as they walked to telephone Evelyn that Rosie's might be a bit noisy for their agenda. After a quick conversation, they'd selected the pizza place on the south side of town.

He glanced at Marjorie as she glanced out the window. "Nice necklace."

"My mom left it to me."

He jolted.

"It's so cool to hear those words."

Marjorie giggled and held up her left arm. "And she left me this watch too."

"This is all a really good freaky."

"I want to tell you before we get there."

She sat up, then grabbed his right hand from the steering wheel and clung to it.

"My mom was named Carol Mullins. She and my dad met at a diner near his base. My dad is Troy Darden."

He stared at her until he felt the car swerve into the oncoming lane and had to jerk it back in place.

"Troy Darden?" Had he shouted?

"Yes. I warned you that you wouldn't believe it."

If Valene weren't behind him, he'd pull over and hear every mind-blowing detail.

"Darlin, your grandmother is right here in Hazel."

"Yes, the cantankerous Wanda Darden."

"Marjorie, I'm dumbfounded."

Carol Mullins.

He glanced at her and somehow, she read his thought.

"They never got a chance to marry."

He stuck his arm out the window to indicate exiting the freeway. The restaurant lay just ahead.

"Does that matter to you?"

"Maybe. Maybe not. One day I may figure that out. But right now, all that matters is that my mother loved me and wanted me."

"Her heart knew what mine does."

Daniel shut off the convertible and could see Valene emerging from her car. He pulled Marjorie against him and held her, then kissed her lips.

Finally.

"Valene's here. You ready for this?"

"I'm ready."

The restaurant lights were dim, supported at each table by candles burning in red jars covered with white netting. The artist in him made him notice such things more than the average guy, but tonight his observance became less about details and more about a sense of privacy. A hostess welcomed them and agreed to Daniel's request for the back booth. She lay three menus on the table. "Enjoy your meal."

He guided Marjorie into the booth, then continued to stand while Valene situated herself on the opposite side. He then slid close to Marjorie and grasped her hand which rested on the envelope between them.

The waiter delivered glasses of water and took their order. As he headed back toward the kitchen, Marjorie pulled out the envelope.

"Valene, my mom was named Carol Mullins."

Marjorie repeated what she'd already told him.

Valene slumped onto the table. "I cannot believe it. I cannot believe it. Poor, lonely Wanda had family all this time." She took hold of Marjorie's hands. "And you, sweet, sweet dear, had a family all along."

Marjorie swiped at her own tears while Valene pulled her napkin from her lap and did the same.

"Marjorie, I don't know whether to feel regret or happiness. I suppose I feel a little of both." Valene's hand rested over her heart.

"I understand, Valene. You sound like my mother in her letter. However, I've decided to go with happy."

She released her hand from Daniel's grip and poured the envelope's contents on the table. Several aged letters, a birth certificate, and a velvet drawstring bag lay before them.

"My mom explained the story in this letter." She lifted one to her chest. "If y'all don't mind, I'll read it."

Marjorie unfolded a letter.

My precious Marjorie,

The thought of you reading this letter makes me feel happy and sad at the same time. I'm happy knowing that you've grown into a young woman. I'm sad realizing I was not there living life beside you. You need to know that was not by choice.

Daniel's nose leaked, and he grabbed his napkin. Marjorie's voice was controlled and...excited. Across from them, Valene's lip quivered.

I hope that one day you can forgive my absence and the absence of your father. I want to tell you our story.

Your father and I loved each other very much. We met at a diner near the base where he was stationed. I worked at the local goods store and had slipped in for coffee and pie after my shift. He came alone, eased onto the stool next to mine, and introduced himself as Private Troy Darden. Do you believe in love at first sight?

Marjorie paused and looked at him. "Yes."

I didn't believe in it until we met. Your father had dark brown hair, almost auburn, and large green eyes. His smile covered his entire face. He really was tall, dark, and handsome. He said my jet-black hair and blue eyes mesmerized him from the start.

Daniel gasped. Her mother had the same effect on Troy that Marjorie had on him.

From that point on, we were together whenever his schedule would allow, which was not often. One day he proposed and I said no. I had to tell him the truth about my future. I have a disease called leukemia. The world may know more about it in your time than it does in mine. But I am dying.

We gave ourselves to one another that day. I know it was wrong, but I don't regret it, because it brought you into the world and let me experience time with the man I loved.

Troy reported for duty soon after that, and we haven't seen each other since. I later learned I was pregnant. We wrote each other for months, and when I wrote that I was pregnant, he proposed again in a letter.

One day, his letters stopped. I will never know why for sure.

I named you Marjorie Grace Mullins because I loved the sound of your first name on my lips. Your middle name was your father's idea. He wrote that he loved that name.

As I write this, you are sleeping next to me in a motel bed. I kept you to myself for a year rather than giving you up, but today that has to change. That year passed without word from Troy. I am so sorry you will never know him. I doubt you will remember our life together in the room I rented above the goods store where I worked. We were accepted in that small world, though I don't know why, but am very grateful.

I think you look like your father, except you have my coloring. As you sleep, I kiss your little nose, eyes, mouth, and ears. You clutched my fingers as I rubbed your hand. That touch will give me the courage I need for my last hours here on earth.

I styled your thick, black hair this morning. I could hardly speak, but I told you over and over how much I love you and will miss you. I hope those words seeped into your heart and you've heard them all your life.

The pain of my heart breaking is worse than the disease.

I have no one to give you to. I'm an only child of only children--all kin have gone on before me. That saddens me more now than ever.

Troy never spoke of his family. I'm not sure why. Whenever I asked, he said he'd introduce me in person. I only knew he came from Hazel and was an only child. I cannot find his kin.

So, today I am leaving you at an orphanage in his home town. I beg God to let you be loved by another family.

I've included your birth certificate, but I did not list Troy as your father because I do not know why he stopped writing me. The letters your father mailed me are yours now. They will support all that I've written here.

I'm also leaving you two items precious to me. The silver necklace belonged to my mother, who died when I was ten.

Marjorie's hand touched the pearl.

The watch is my favorite one. I love watches.

Marjorie raised her left arm. "This one. I love watches too." A whimper escaped her and settled in Daniel's heart.

My life has been pretty simple. Daddy took us to church every time he could. I grew up an only child, went to school, then started working at the goods store. After hours, I did hair and nails in the back of the store to earn extra money. I guess I got that knack from my mother, because I recall her giving haircuts and coloring hair of her friends in our kitchen.

Valene released a blubbery "Oh my goodness."

Daniel bragged, "Your talent came from both sides of your family."

My father passed when I was eighteen, just a couple of years before you came along. He would have loved you very much.

Don't feel ashamed of your beginning. I asked God to forgive me and at the same time thanked him for you. I hope you love Jesus. He has always loved you.

You were a wiggly child in my womb and stayed that way after you were born. I imagine that as a sign you'd be full of sparkle all your life.

My darling girl, I am so sorry for any sadness my absence has brought you. I am so, so sorry that I deserted you. I can only hope that your coming in to this world has brightened the lives of others like it brightened mine.

I love you. I want you. I miss you.

Carol Ruth Mullins, Mother.

P.S. The contents of this envelope were to remain sealed until you became old enough to understand and choose to read them.

The waiter arrived with their pizza and said nothing as he placed it on the table. Daniel eyed him. "Thank you."

The break in the emotion was welcomed. He served the slices while Valene admired the jewelry and rubbed her hands over the letter.

Daniel hesitated to ask a question, but did anyway.

"So, why do you think you were never adopted?"

"Miss Bords thought maybe because I was not a newborn. Then I probably grew too old. I was just never chosen."

Her brow wrinkled.

Daniel took a sip, then hugged her shoulder. "You might not be here with us if you'd been adopted." He whistled. "Man, not cool. What a selfish thing for me to say." He felt his face heat up.

Marjorie swallowed. "I'm glad you feel that way. I realize now that God didn't have to figure this out. He already knew what He planned for me."

"Your story is beautiful." Marjorie's boss sniffled.

"Valene, you'll have to tell me when and how to tell Wanda. I'm excited, but scared after seeing her so weak."

"Don't be scared. I think joy will return to her life. It will be as though Troy has come home in spirit and brought a treasure. Let me think about when, since you asked."

Marjorie looked at Daniel. "I'm overwhelmed. In the best way."

He placed his piece of pizza on the plate and swiped at his mouth. "Of course you are. But Darlin', lots of people in your life will help you through this." He tweaked her nose. "They'll just have to wait in line behind me to do so."

She giggled, then pushed the remaining letters toward him. "Pick one."

"Oh, Marjorie, no. You read what you want us to hear."

"Ok, we'll start with this one."

He noted the masculine writing on the yellowed envelope. Did other men notice those things or did he because he spent half his life cyphering junior high penmanship? Seeing Troy's name felt surreal. Time existed when Troy Darden had not been MIA or a deceased war hero, but just an ordinary man in love.

Marjorie took a bite and sip, then wiped her hands and began to read.

My darling Carol,

We're expecting a child! And it's coming the week before my birthday. My heart is bursting. I whooped and shouted when I read the news. I am already a proud father. Sweetheart, I ask you again, will you marry me when I return? We'll go to the justice of the peace and hurry things along. I only need a yes. I don't need to be reminded that your life may be cut short.

Whatever time we can have together is worth it. The three of us will be a family. Is it a girl or a boy? I guess you don't know that. What do you think about Grace? I love that name. Or Troy Junior?

Please rest. I reckon this is hard on your body. If I could take that rotten disease from you, I would.

I will never regret the time we loved one another. I hope that you don't either. I do regret our not getting married. We made a baby. Jeepers, I still can't get over that. I'm grinning from one ear to the other. I wish I was there to help you and watch our baby grow inside. Now don't you go pouting about a growing belly. I imagine it is a beautiful sight.

I am sorry you will bear the shame of being an unwed mother. I should be there beside you. Please don't go into one of those homes and give up our baby. Maybe that is selfish of me, but I want to be the daddy of our child when I return. Can you bear up somehow until I return?

I will write my family at some point, after I get your yes, and tell them all about the THREE of us.

You are in my thoughts every moment. Every day I pray for my gal, and now our baby. I love you.

Your adoring, madly in love, soon to be husband,

Troy

A silence settled over the table. Marjorie's unopened life had been revealed, and she'd been wanted and loved from the very beginning.

21

Marjorie swallowed around the lump in her throat. She didn't want to spew her lunch right here in the hospital hallway. For more than a week, she'd held back from telling Wanda Darden that she was her granddaughter. She'd visited her only a couple of times, thinking more visits would seem weird to Wanda. At last, both she and Valene agreed the woman was healthy and alert enough to absorb the news.

"Daniel, I'm scared."

He stilled their pace and placed the envelope under his arm. He grabbed the hand he wasn't holding. The hand she hoped would bear an engagement ring soon.

"Sweetheart, Valene wouldn't set you up for a disaster. Wanda is ready to meet her granddaughter."

When Daniel pulled her into an embrace and whispered a prayer in her ear, a sense of peace came over her, along with the desire to kiss him—the man smelled so good. He pulled away, then guided her forward.

"God's looking down and smiling, Marjorie."

"And maybe Momma and Daddy too." She squeezed his hand.

Her life had become richer in the last several weeks through work, school, love, friends, family, and God. He'd watched over her even when she intentionally shunned Him. All along, he'd been working to bring her to this hallway with this man to hug her grandmother.

She sighed.

The door to Wanda's room rested slightly ajar. She could see Valene sitting next to the bed flipping through a magazine.

Daniel tapped on the door with his knuckle.

"Come in."

Grandmother.

Her grandmother was welcoming her inside the room.

Oh, please, welcome me inside your heart.

Marjorie scooted past the man she loved and entered, his essence surrounding her as he followed her into the room.

Marjorie stood at the foot of the bed, her legs bouncing with emotion.

"My grandchild." Wanda's hand reached toward her as far as wires allowed. "You look just like your Daddy. I don't know how I never saw it until this moment. The heart has eyes."

Tears rolled down Marjorie's cheeks as she moved to take her grandmother's hand. The touch made her heart thud against her chest.

"Hello, Grandmother." Her emotions could curl up and cry or jump and shout. Marjorie squealed. This meeting was a celebration.

Two souls longed for one another for years. Two lives, connected by blood, had passed each other, yet smiled as strangers. An orphaned child had grieved. A lonely mother had mourned. Today was a day of birth. A new family was formed.

"I love you." And she did, with her entire heart. "I've missed you all my life."

"Honey, I didn't know. I didn't know. I wouldn't have deserted you. If I'd known about you, I'd have raised you. This old heart had lots of love to share, but instead it fermented into orneriness and spewed out of me. I love you already. I do."

Marjorie kissed the aged hand.

"Do you want to be called Grandmother?" She looked at Wanda and smiled.

"I always dreamed of being a grandma."

Wanda cried. Just a few weeks ago, Marjorie would have sworn the tough woman would be incapable of such emotion. She gently wiped the tears from her grandmother's cheeks. "Grandma it is."

"I see your fine young man is here. Son, you have my blessing to marry my granddaughter. No need to fiddle with formalities."

Marjorie gasped, and Valene chortled.

Her Daniel threw his head back and guffawed.

"Grandma, you want to read your son's letters? Hear from the woman he loved?"

Daniel pulled two chairs to the bed.

Wanda's lips released a whimper that formed a sob. Marjorie leaned against her gently. Maybe now she could truly mourn her son and put him to rest in the most basic of human ways, with no formality, and surrounded by people who loved her.

When the moment passed, Marjorie pulled out the contents of the envelope and laid them in Wanda's lap. Her aged hand, still perfectly manicured, rubbed the treasures. She lifted a letter to her lips and kissed it, then breathed in its scent.

"My boy."

"My Daddy."

Wanda opened a letter and handed it to her. For the next several minutes, Troy's words came through the voice of his daughter.

As she placed the last letter back into the envelope, Wanda took her hand.

"Marjorie, I know why Troy never talked about his family. It was just the two of us for years, and I had such high expectations for him. Never considered his talents, his preferences. Already had a match in mind for him, and he knew it. When he left for the military, we parted on unfriendly terms. I got three letters from him. None filled with emotion like I just heard. Just facts. If he wrote more, they never got here or were lost forever. I robbed myself of my own son."

"Wanda, you don't have to carry that pain anymore." Valene rubbed the woman's shoulders.

"Grandma, we've both had our share of pain. We've grieved tonight. We'll grieve again I suppose. But this is a celebration. You and I have a future."

Wanda grinned. "You and I and that young man who's yet to admit to me he loves you."

Daniel stood, pulled Marjorie to him and kissed her right there in front of Grandma.

"I love her."

• • •

Marjorie rubbed her ankle, then rested her head against Daniel's shoulder. Her pink chiffon dress was adorned with Daniel's suit jacket. He shifted on the blanket he'd laid out for them at the pond.

"The dance was a success. You'll never get off that committee."

"I'll have to plan a disaster for next year if that's the case." He kissed her hair.

"I still can't get over the Dance Do. The receptionist at the school has already asked me for next year's date. I can't wait to see the ad in the yearbook."

"The girls looked real nice tonight. Very pretty. But I feel freaky saying that."

She giggled. "Great idea from the amazing Mr. Buckler. I repeat, 'You'll never get off that dance committee.'"

"Mmm hmm." His voice was deep, distracted, and filled with desire. She lifted her head and looked Daniel in the eyes. The darkness didn't hide the intensity, and her being felt the impact of his gaze.

"I love you, Marjorie."

Always and forever.

"I love you too, Daniel."

Always and forever.

"This very spot is where God told me what a doofus I was planning to be that weekend I ended up traveling to Austin."

"I'm glad those-whose-names-I-will-not-say returned to Louisiana together."

"Me too."

She touched his cheek. "And I recall you saying you took care of an errand that weekend in Austin."

"You recall correctly."

Daniel shifted to his knees and pulled a small box from his pants pocket and opened it. "Will you marry me, Marjorie Grace Mullins?"

"I will." No need to let a split-second pass between the question and the answer.

He slid the ring onto her perfectly manicured finger, then leaned into her. His weight pushed her body against the ground, but the kiss lingered as his upper torso lay against hers. The situation felt precarious and desirous—and beautiful, just as God intended.

No wonder I was born.

Daniel gathered his wits, and swooped her into his arms. "Think on that for a while, soon-to-be-Mrs. Buckler."

Something shifted inside her, and she could swear her whole self opened up with sheer joy.

THE END

EPILOGUE

June 1962

Daniel opened the passenger door of Marjorie's new blue Impala, then looked at her and smiled.

"Do you want me to take the baby?"

She lifted a bundle and pressed her lips against a tiny, fuzzy head and kissed it before handing the bundle to him. Daniel nestled the newborn against his chest before positioning it in the crook of one arm. The child yawned, and Daniel felt his entire face smile. *I'm a father.*

He offered his free hand to Marjorie and gently helped her rise from the seat. How his stunning wife had become more lovely than the day he'd first laid eyes on her standing on the sidewalk, he couldn't fathom. But she had. His heart thudded against his chest.

She stood and hooked her arm through his free one. The car door, flowers, cards, and suitcase would have to wait. His arms were filled with his family. Together they moved along the sidewalk to enter the house they recently purchased. A large ribbon adorned the front door that was keeping all their family at bay. He'd asked that Marjorie and the baby be able to enter inside before all the "oohs and aahs" and my-turn-to-hold started. His eyes roamed the street curb and noted whose cars were parked outside the house. He smiled. His step-mother had done well—judging from the cars, just immediate family appeared to be inside the walls of their home.

When they reached the door, he handed Marjorie the baby then kissed them both.

"Are you two ready for this?"

"We are." Marjorie's eyes twinkled as their gazes met.

Daniel breathed with contentment. Overhead the sun shined upon them while gardenia bushes in the yard offered a sweet fragrance, and somewhere in the distance birds tweeted— nature's lullaby.

He turned the knob, then eased his family through the door-way. "We're home."

Like a breeze passing through, family stood one after the other and adorations filled the air as Daniel paused for a moment and let relatives admire his wife and child. Dad, Tali, Theo, Lucy, and Valene filled the space around them.

From the corner of his eye, he spotted a tray of sandwiches and other foods laid out on decorated kitchen table.

"Oh, in person is so much better than peeking through the hospital nursery windows." Lucy Buckler patted her son's arm as she spoke.

"Little Sweet Precious." The moniker came from Theo.

The child squeaked as though saying hello to kin.

To his left, Daniel's eye was drawn to the portrait of Marjorie hanging on the back wall of their den. When he'd started the piece, she still didn't know anything about her family. How life had changed.

Daniel guided his family to the one person who had yet to see his child. Wanda Darden was seated in the rocker next to the couch. She'd not risen when they walked in, and now Daniel could see why. Tears rolled down the woman's cheeks and her shoulders shook. As his new family approached her, she smiled.

"I'm just overcome with joy. These tears have been stored up for too many years."

Marjorie removed her arm from his, then offered the bundle to Wanda.

"Grandma, meet Troy Darden Buckler."

Overwhelming joy filled Daniel for his wife. She'd opened her life and found family in the here and now, the past, and for years to come.

AUTHOR NOTES

I hope you enjoyed getting to know Marjorie and Daniel as much as I did. Thank you for reading my stories. My mom was a beautician and worked for a while in the salon of an assisted living home. That scenario was the starting point for this story.

Much happened in life as I wrote this book. The world experienced a pandemic. I and other family members fell ill. I thank God that we all survived the illness and extend condolences to those who lost loved ones in the pandemic. My husband and I gained three more grandchildren, with our fifth one due before the release of this book. They all live within three miles of us. We are blessed. I experienced my first broken bone and couldn't resist including a bit of the hassle in the story.

I wish to thank my readers who waited patiently for this book. You played a part in the writing by participating in my social media conversations. I kept track, and readers gave input on seventeen different questions or inquiries. A special thanks to Donna Burroughs, who offered the name Rosie's for a diner. As it turned out, one of my grandchildren is also named Rosie, making the name sentimental as well as fitting. Thanks to LeeAnn Carpenter for allowing me to use the nickname "Pie Lady," which is a sweet reference to her mother. Tali Belokonny gave me permission to use her beautiful name in a story. I thought it was a good fit for Daniel's spunky stepsister. My hair stylist, Kim Boyett, was a crutch I leaned on while writing about the beauty shop and beauty school Thank you, Kim, for all your valuable input, expertise, details, and stories. You made me smile as we conversed about this project while you hid my gray.

My heartfelt thanks goes to the team who supported the production of this book. Janette, your input as my beta reader helped make the story richer. Jeanette, my editor, thank you for your honesty and support. Your eyes saw things mine would never catch. Wendy, thank you for proofing my work to find the typos and contradictions that resulted from my editing phase. I had utmost confidence in your skills and input. It has been a pleasure to work with Tara at Teaberry Creative. Your talent made the book visually appealing.

My husband, Lynn, kept me motivated. He supported me through times of frustration. He gave input when I asked him for it. He put up with my closed door as I pounded on the keyboard. This book would not have become a reality without his encouragement. I love you.

To my children and grandchildren—you make me happy.

To God and my Savior, thank you for never giving up on me and for giving me the desire to write. My desire is to honor you with this work of fiction.

I enjoy staying in touch with readers. You can email me at kimwilliamsbook@gmail.com and follow me on Facebook, Amazon, and Instagram. My website is www.kimwilliamsbook.com.

I invite you to read and share my Letters to Layton Series found on Amazon or at my website.

OTHER BOOKS BY KIM WILLIAMS

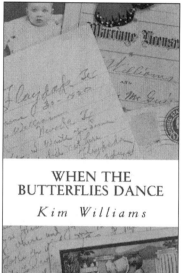

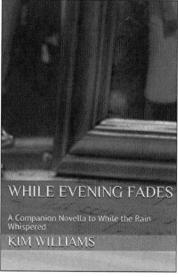

Made in the USA
Columbia, SC
17 May 2022

60536703R00154